Nobody Told ME
I was A QueeN

Nobody Told ME
I was A QueeN

PJ RICHARDSON

Cover Design by Edward Mills
New Millennium Creatures

authorHOUSE®

AuthorHouse™
1663 Liberty Drive
Bloomington, IN 47403
www.authorhouse.com
Phone: 1-800-839-8640

Published by AuthorHouse   09/30/2014

ISBN: 978-1-4817-2897-3 (sc)
ISBN: 978-1-4817-2896-6 (e)

Library of Congress Control Number: 2013904746

To All My Beautiful Sisters,
This one is for you!

CHAPTER ONE

Roberta

"Bobbi are you coming to the restaurant this evening?"

"Of course Amanda I will be there. You are serving my favorite dish today right?"

"Quit lying girl! You know damn well you hate ox tails. I remember what you wrote about my ox tails in your little article."

"Did I ever tell you how sorry I was about that?"

"Forget you Bobbi! You better be glad you are my friend now."

We both started laughing. Amanda and I are friends now. In fact we are the best of friends. I guess every time we think of the strange way we became friends we can't do anything but laugh.

I work as a food and restaurant critic for our local newspaper and Amanda owns the only upscale soul food restaurant in our city.

One day I had to critique her place for the newspaper's weekend review. On this particular day Amanda decided that since I was African-American, I would appreciate a good pot of ox tail stew. Wrong! I wrote that the restaurant was beautiful and very cozy, (which was a surprise for a soul food place) but the stew was not one of my favorites. I also wrote that she should have low calorie meals along with her regular meals so customers can have a choice and not just food full of calories and cholesterol. But otherwise I was really impressed with her restaurant.

Ms. Walker's Soul Food Cuisine is Amanda's restaurant that she inherited after her parents died. It was called "Soul Food Cuisine" until Amanda took over and changed everything. When I say upscale, it really is. On the weekend you have to make reservations to get in that puppy. She has a small jazz band that plays on Friday and Saturday nights until 1:00am and there is also a bar on one side with couches and recliners so you can listen to the music and just relax as if you were in your own place. Amanda says that just because its soul food that doesn't mean it has to look like a diner. She says that most people think soul food is the cheap food that poor black folks eat. So she decided to get away from that image and she really has.

Her food is not cheap at all. Even the cornbread that is placed on the table before the meal is served on a beautiful silver platter. Most people who use to frequent her parent's place were skeptical when she took over. But they have all come around. Now people come from near and far to eat at her place. In fact, this is my Friday night hang out. This is where I meet Amanda and our other friend Colleen every Friday night.

"Yes of course I will be there. After the week I've had I need a hard stiff one."

"I hope you are talking about a drink because that's the only stiff one you're going to get at my spot."

"Yes I am! What did you think I was talking about Amanda?"

"I don't know girl. Maybe you thought Darnell was going to be here tonight."

"Amanda I am so over Darnell."

"Quit lying to yourself Bobbi. Remember who you are talking to."

"I am not lying to myself or you. I have to be over him. I can't continue to go through this shit with his ass."

"I know Bobbi he has put you through a lot. But I thought this time he was going to treat you differently."

"Why because he came back begging and crying and talking about how he has changed this time and he will never leave me again?"

"I believed him Bobbi. He had me convinced."

"Yeah I was convinced too Amanda. Things were going great until he took my car, my money, and my credit cards and went crazy."

"You did report his black ass to the police right?"

"Of course I did. They caught him and girl you know when I got to the police station he had the nerve to be down there tripping and calling me out my name."

"That's some shit! Why is he mad at you when he did you wrong?"

"I know it's crazy. But the crazy part of all this is he had the nerve to call me from the station later that night."

"You didn't accept his call did you Bobbi?"

"Yeah I did."

"Bobbi! Why would you do that? After all that shit he put you through." Amanda yelled.

"I know Amanda! Stop yelling!" I yelled back.

"I'm sorry Bobbi for yelling at you. I just don't want you to be hurt anymore by that creep."

"I understand Amanda. I didn't say I am taking him back. I just listened to what he had to say. I guess I sort of felt sorry for him."

"Sorry for him!" She yelled again. "When is someone going to feel sorry for us? Here I am running a business and raising two kids without a man in the house and with very little time left for myself. When is someone going to feel sorry for me?"

"Why do you say that Amanda? I think you have a good life? You own and operate a successful business. You are raising two wonderful kids and you live in a big beautiful home."

"And I don't have a man. Remember my husband left with that young woman at the church."

"I'm sorry Amanda. I almost forgot."

"See now you feel sorry for me." She said as if she was proving a point.

"Well enough of that. Have you talked to Colleen today? Is she coming this evening?" I said changing the subject.

"Yes she is coming. I talked to her this morning after she did the morning news. Did you see her this morning?"

"Yeah I caught the news this morning. I am going to have to talk to her about her new hairdresser. Her hair is too long to have it up in that bun."

"I sort of liked it."

"You would. I have to go. I'll see you later around 7:30."

"Cool I'll see you then."

We both hung up. I didn't intend to talk to her that long, but sometimes Amanda can go on and on. And I know I need to get my ass to the newspaper.

I have been working there for seven years in the same position. Senior Food Critic is my job title. (I don't know why they call me senior. I am the only food critic there.)

Don't get me wrong, I love my job. I get to eat at nice restaurants and when I am not working I get invited to different restaurants all over the city. Sometimes I take Amanda and Colleen with me. They love it. Although Colleen is the star, I get more star treatment when it comes to dinner invitations than she does. I think that makes her a little jealous sometimes. She would never admit it though.

Colleen is the morning news anchor for station KACW TV 12. It is a station here locally in our beautiful city of Minneapolis. Colleen is half African-American and half Native American. We tease her sometimes about how she looks on camera. In certain light she could easily pass for white. She hates when we say that. Not that she is prejudice in any way. She just likes who she is and her own culture.

I met Colleen when the station had me on as a guest. I was on to talk about being a Food Critic and how exciting it can be. After the show she invited me out for coffee. We talked for hours and that was the start of a great friendship. We realized that we had so much in common. Even our childhoods were similar. The only difference was that she has a stressful job and I am more relaxed at my job than people could ever imagine.

I guess her job is stressful because she has to compete and be more competent than her male counterparts. Another thing we have in common is the fact that we both have had "no-good-men" in our lives.

CHAPTER TWO

Roberta

By the end of the day I was ready to hang with my girls and have a drink. I am not a big drinker, but on Fridays with my girls you would think that I was a seasoned drunk.

I made it to the restaurant at 7:30 exactly. I know I beat Colleen here because she has to always drop that smart ass sixteen year old daughter of hers off somewhere. Sometimes I wish Colleen would just smack her in her fucking mouth when she talks back. When I was growing up we couldn't give our parents "word-for-word". I know my mother would have knocked the shit out of any of her kids if we ever tried that with her. But Colleen is different with Sabrina.

"Hey sweetie!" I said as soon as I walked into the lounge area. I was talking to Amanda's handsome bartender.

"Hello Bobbi! You look like a million bucks!" He said. "What will it be? The usual I presume?"

"Joe you know I don't have a usual. I just drink whatever Amanda and Colleen is drinking."

"Well tonight Ms. Cotton you are drinking Cosmos."

"Why? Is Amanda having one of those days?"

"Yes she is. But it's cool. She'll be fine. She just needs to kick back with her girls and relax that's all."

"Why is it Joe that you seem to always know what Amanda needs?"

"That's part of my job to keep the boss happy." He said while making my drink.

"Your job is to be the bartender and manager."

"That is part of being a bartender and manager. Looking out for the boss's needs and making sure she is taken care of."

"I guess maybe you're right."

He handed me my drink.

"I am going to sit right over there near the stage. Can you point Amanda and Colleen in my direction when you see them please?"

"You got it sexy." He said.

I took my drink and headed to my favorite seat near the stage. I love sitting there but Colleen says it's too close to the stage. The band is too loud and she can't hear herself think she says.

"Don't drink that too fast. You know you can't hold your liquor. You're going to mess around and get drunk."

"Hey Girl, I knew I would beat your slow ass here." I said as I stood up to hug Colleen.

"I would have been here sooner, but you know Sabrina had somewhere she needed me to drop her at. I promise I am going to get that girl a car soon. And I knew you would pick these seats. Bobbi you always have to be in the center of things."

"Sit down Colleen and these seats are fine."

"Yeah they're fine for you. But I'm older than you and my hearing is not as good as yours." Colleen said laughing.

"You are only two years older than I am."

"Two years is a lot."

"Shut up Colleen and go over to the bar and get a drink."

"Where's the waitress?" She asked looking around.

"I don't know. Just go get Joe to make you a Cosmo."

"Are we drinking Cosmos? Is Amanda having one of them days?"

"Yes I believe she is."

"Maybe she's upset about getting those divorce papers yesterday."

"She didn't tell me anything about any divorce papers. Colleen are you sure?"

"Hell yeah I'm sure. Wait a minute Bobbi. I'll be right back." She said and walked over to the bar.

Dang, why didn't Amanda tell me that that "no-good" husband of hers was filing for divorce? And why did she tell Colleen and not me? I hope that was just an oversight on her part. Because we both know that Colleen can't keep a secret to save her life.

Amanda walked in the lounge and looked around. She looked over at Colleen talking to Joe at the bar and then turned and looked toward the stage where I was sitting and headed in my direction.

Amanda is so beautiful. Just looking at her walking towards me, if I didn't know any better, I would easily mistake her for a model or even a supermodel. She is five feet seven inches and has a body like she works out every day. But she doesn't. She may run around her neighborhood once a week but that's it. But Colleen and I are at the gym four to five times a week. We don't have the luxury of waking up and looking good like Amanda does.

"Girl I am so glad that you guys are here. I really need my girls with me right now." Amanda said. We both hug tightly.

"Amanda why didn't you tell me that you got divorce papers?"

"I was going to tell you but we started talking about something else. I guess Colleen told you."

"Yes I did!" Colleen said as soon as she walked over to the table. You bitches know I can't hold any news. I am a reporter remember?"

"Sit your news reporting ass down." Amanda said laughing.

Now all three of us were together again on this Friday night kicking it! It just doesn't seem like the week is complete unless we end it together. I hope this is our tradition for the rest of our lives.

We talked for hours about how our week was going and how things could have been better. In between talking there was drinking and eating hot wings, potato skins, and the best catfish I have ever tasted. Amanda has great food here and we were putting it away like it was our last meal. We sat there eating and talking stuff for hours. I know all of us were on our third drink. Maybe Colleen was on her fourth.

"You know what your problem is Amanda?" Colleen asked.

"Why every time your ass start drinking, you want to tell me and Amanda "what our problem is?" I chimed in.

"Be quiet Bobbi because your ass is next." Colleen said which made us all start laughing.

"Amanda you need to lose your temper on that husband of yours. Excuse me, I mean that "soon-to-be" ex-husband of yours."

"Why do I need to do that Colleen?"

"Yeah why does she need to do that?" I asked.

"You just sit and chill Bobbi because I'm getting to you next." She said laughing.

"Tell me Colleen, how is losing my temper going to help me?"

"Wait a minute. That's my jam! I love that song! I love when Jonathon Butler does "Fire and Rain!" She said shaking her head and snapping her fingers. You could tell Colleen had had too much to drink.

"I thought you didn't like sitting this close to the stage Colleen. And that is not Jonathon Butler up there singing." I said.

"I know that Bobbi. I am just saying that I love this song. And for your information I don't like sitting this close, but this band is great!"

"You're drunk!" Amanda said laughing. We were all laughing.

"I'm not drunk! I just feel good tonight. I love hanging with you guys."

"Girl shut-up and get back to why I need to lose my temper."

"You need to go mid-evil on his ass! And you need to book this band every Friday. If you do that then I promise I will be here every week."

"Girl shut up! You are here every week anyway fool!" I said. Again we were all laughing so hard we could hardly talk.

It is so good to see Colleen so relaxed with her hair down. She so often has to be in control all the time. And not to mention how she had to be when her husband was alive. It's amazing that she is able to laugh and be happy now. It's amazing her and her daughter are able to live again.

Colleen has one daughter named Sabrina who is sixteen. Colleen was married to a very abusive man. He cheated on her and every time she would catch him he would get mad at her and start a fight with her. He would hit her, kick her or even spit in her face. I always wondered why she just wouldn't take her daughter and just leave. Amanda and I often told her she could come and stay with either one of us at any time she wanted. But she always declined. She said she never wanted to get us involved in her mess. She would simply say that she could handle it and that she had a plan. She didn't know that every time we saw a bruise on her face Amanda and I would cry together.

After years of being beat and going to work and having her make-up artist hide her facial flaws, her husband Morris had a massive heart attack and died. His life insurance was large so Colleen was able to pay off their house.

I remember Colleen saying once that if he hadn't died of a heart attack that she was going to kill him. Amanda and I often joke about Colleen killing her husband. Maybe that was her plan all along.

"Colleen it's time for you to go home. I think you've had way too much to drink." Amanda said. "Remember you are a star in this town."

"Yeah, Amanda's right Colleen. Let's go because it's starting to get too crowded anyway." I said.

"Okay! Okay! Just let me go to the bathroom first." She said.

"Go and hurry the fuck up! We can walk out together. I need to get home."

"For what bitch, no one's there." She said laughing. We were all still laughing. Colleen walked away toward the restroom.

"Amanda what do you think Colleen was taking about when she told you to lose your temper?"

"I don't know Bobbi. I don't listen to Colleen when she is drunk. What does she know anyway? She let a man beat the hell out of her for years."

"Well she did get tired of him and eventually killed his ass."

We gave each other a hi-five and fell back in our seats laughing.

"What the hell are you two Heifers laughing at?" Colleen asked when she walked from the restroom.

"Nothing." I said and stood up. "Let's go."

"Well Amanda it has been another wonderful evening." Colleen said while hugging Amanda. "Remember keep that band."

"Yes I totally agree. That band is the bomb." I said while giving my hugs. We both walked out the lounge and headed out the door to where our cars were parked.

"Are you sure you can drive Colleen?"

"Yes Girl I can drive. Why do you ask? You can't drive me. You drank as much as I did."

"Yes but I am a better drunk than you are."

"Girl get your ass in your car. I will call you when I make it home."

"Cool. Do that!" I said and we both drove away still laughing.

CHAPTER THREE

Roberta

I drove home that night still thinking about how much fun I had hanging with my girls. Every time we get together we always have a good time laughing at with each other. It seems that I live for my Friday nights.

When I pulled up in my apartment complex, I could see that there must be someone having a party or something because there were cars parked everywhere. I was hoping that no one was in my space because I am not in the mood to call security and have them removed. I have had to do this a few times in the past so it is something that I will do in a heartbeat. We have assigned spaces but visitors are not aware of that and they tend to park wherever there is an open spot.

Just like I thought, someone was parked in my space. Damn! Now I have to call security. But as I pull up closer I can see that there is someone sitting in the car smoking a cigarette. It's Darnell and he gets out of the car. I put my car in reverse to get away from his ass.

"Wait Roberta, please don't pull off!" He yelled.

I stopped my car. Why? I don't know.

"Darnell what are you doing here?"

"Roberta I got out of jail yesterday and I just wanted to see you."

"Darnell why are you here really?"

"Roberta can I come in and talk to you for a minute?"

"We have nothing to talk about. You are not someone I can trust."

"Please Roberta don't say stuff like that. Baby I made a mistake but I love you."

"Darnell you don't love me! You don't treat people you love like you treat me. Please move that car so I can park in my space and go in my apartment." I yelled.

"Sure Baby, I'll move the car. But can I please come in and explain myself?"

"No Darnell and I can't keep going through this shit with you."

"We are only going through stuff that couples go through Roberta."

"No Darnell that's not true. Most couples don't have to deal with the other person stealing money, credit cards, and their car."

"Can you please just let me explain what I was going through at that time when I made those terrible mistakes?"

"What about everything I had to go through Darnell? I couldn't get to work and I felt so stupid talking to the police about this. Man fuck this! Move that car Darnell before I smash it and you too!" I was mad all over again.

"Okay, okay." He said and jumped in his car.

As soon as he pulled out, I pulled my car in.

Darnell has a lot of nerves coming here. I should have gotten a restraining order on him. How did I ever get involved with this man?

I met Darnell Nunn one afternoon after having lunch at this small restaurant down town. I was walking to my car when this very handsome brown skinned man appeared behind me. At first I thought that he was following me, but when I turned and looked in his face and saw how fine he was, I sure hoped he was following me. He was gorgeous and when he smiled that said it all.

"Excuse me, but I just couldn't help but notice you in the restaurant sitting there all by yourself." He said.

"That's funny I hadn't noticed you in the restaurant. Where were you sitting?" I asked because I really hadn't seen him there. The way he looked, I would have remembered.

"I was in the kitchen. I am the assistant to the Chef. I was finishing up my shift when I saw you sitting there all by yourself. So tell me why a woman that looks like you would be having lunch alone?"

"First of all, I often eat alone. I am a Food and Restaurant Critic. I don't mind having meals alone."

"What's your name beautiful?" He asked

"My name is Roberta. But most people call me Bobbi."

"Hello Roberta, my name is Darnell Nunn and I am very pleased to meet you." He said and held out his hand for me to shake.

That conversation ended up lasting for over an hour. We exchanged numbers and the following week we were on our first date. He is a couple years younger than I am, but age is nothing but a number. And besides we really hit it off great.

After that we were together all the time. Shopping, going to the movies, and eating out. And the sex was the bomb! He was one of the best lovers I have ever had. He was gentle and romantic and everything I could ever want in a lover. He made my body do something that no man had ever done before. He is the only man that has ever made me have multiple orgasms. I have to admit, he has the "magic stick".

But soon all of our magic started to dissipate. I don't know what happened. He started lying and always in need of some extra money. Yes, most of the time I gave it to him, but only because I wanted to make him happy. Now I just can't take it anymore and I am not going to.

He followed me into my apartment. I didn't even try to fight with him about coming in.

"Look Darnell I don't know what you're thinking, but I just can't do this anymore." I said as soon as I walked in my living room and sat on my couch.

"Roberta I hate that I hurt you again. How could I be so stupid?"

He got on his knees right next to me. I could feel myself getting weak. Looking in his face while he was on his knees was clearly making me weak.

"Get up Darnell. I can't do this."

"Do what Roberta? Love me?"

"Loving you has never been the problem. You not treating me with love and respect is the problem."

"I do love you. I just do stupid shit. Please forgive me. I need you Roberta."

"You don't act like it."

"I know baby, but if you give me another chance, I promise this time things will be different. I want to have a family. I want you to give me a family."

There it is! Every time he talks about having a baby I just melt. He is the only man that I have ever thought about having a baby with. Hell he is the only man who ever asked me to have his baby.

The next thing I knew we were kissing and Darnell was taking off my clothes. He was kissing and licking every part of my body slowly and with such passion. He was making me feel as if he was really sorry. I think this time he really meant every thing he was saying. We made love right there on the floor of my living room.

After we finished he followed me into the shower where we were at it again. This time I was kissing him all over and I even found myself asking him to stay with me and never leave. I don't know if it was the alcohol or the overwhelming desire to have a man stay with me.

The next morning while I slept Darnell made breakfast and brought it to me in bed. He can be so sweet sometimes. With all this sweetness, I forgot to ask how he got out of jail and whose car he was driving. But fuck it! Things are going too good right now to rock the boat.

The following week Darnell did exactly what he said he would do. He went to work and came straight to me after his shift was over. He continued to talk about having a family and I was convinced that he was trying to get me pregnant. We made love every day sometimes twice a day.

I didn't tell my girls right away about me and Darnell being back together. They both want me to be happy, but they think I am wasting my time with him. I decided that I would tell Colleen first. We were meeting for coffee so I would tell her then.

Colleen likes to have coffee at this shop that has every kind of coffee or tea you could imagine. I don't drink coffee unless its cappuccino, but I love tea.

When we got there Colleen ordered her usual latte and I ordered a mint tea. We decided to sit outside at one of the tables since it was such a nice day.

"Can you believe this weather Bobbi?

"Girl it is wonderful isn't it? This weather makes me feel as if summer is on its way."

"We know we better enjoy it while we can. You know this is Minnesota and it could be snowing tomorrow."

"You are right. So Bobbi what's up? You have been really quiet lately and we haven't heard from you all week."

"Why do you say that?" I said nearly choking on my tea.

"I know you Bobbi and I know when you are up to something. I can just feel it."

"No I'm not. I have just been working and doing things around my apartment."

"Doing what things? Your place is beautiful."

"Well thank-you, but I have been working on a project in my bathroom." I said and took another sip of my tea.

"So have you heard from Darnell?"

Now why did she ask me that question?

"Why did you ask me that Colleen?"

She took a sip of her latte.

"I asked that Bobbi because I know you. And I know that you are weak for him."

"I'm not weak for him Colleen. I just have him in my heart."

She looked around before she said another word. I know her too. She was thinking of something profound to say.

"Say it Colleen. Say that I'm crazy for taking him back. Say how you think I can do so much better."

She was just sitting there looking into the wind.

"Say something Colleen."

"I don't have anything to say Bobbi. Well not about you and Darnell anyway."

"Well what's on your mind?" I asked. She was starting to confuse me.

"I was just thinking. What is it about the three of us that makes us settle for less than we deserve?"

"What do you mean?"

"I'm saying look at Amanda. She was married to a man that cheated on her every chance he got. She stayed until he decided he wanted out. Then look at you."

"What about me?"

"Bobbi you know damn well that Darnell's disappearing acts drive you crazy. But what do you do? You take him back over and over again. Then there's me. I was married to a man who beat me every time he felt like it. I never left or even tried to leave until the end. I truly don't know if I even had the nerve to leave or seek help. All I know is I wanted out but was afraid to make that first step."

We both sat there in silence. I knew Colleen was right, but I wasn't ready to let Darnell go yet. I don't have any other man in my life who knows me like he does. I am comfortable with him and we know how to make each other feel good.

"Just be careful Bobbi. I just care a lot about you and I am tired of seeing you hurt and sad."

I didn't say a word for a minute as we both sipped on our drinks. I then decided to lighten the mood.

"Don't worry about me Colleen. I have a friend that can show me how to kill him and make it look like a heart attack."

"Oh fuck you Bobbi!"

We both started laughing.

CHAPTER FOUR

Amanda

This restaurant seems to be getting busier and busier. I don't remember it ever being this busy everyday of the week when my parents owned it. Don't get me wrong, I am very grateful for all of the business. It keeps me so busy that I don't have time to worry about my problems.

A lot of my customers are the same customers that my parents had. Some of them even tell me that my meals are the best they have ever eaten. Even though I serve some of the same meals my parents served. My presentation is just different.

My parents started this restaurant when they moved here from Mississippi. My father was working as a construction worker and during lunch time, he would always share some of his lunch with his coworkers. His lunch always consisted of meat and potatoes and some type of dessert.

After a while, his coworkers, and even his foreman, would put orders in for my mother to make cakes, pies, or even cater weddings and holidays. One day my father thought that they would make more money if they opened a restaurant of their own. At first, my mother was not even interested in owning a restaurant. She would say that she couldn't run a restaurant and a home. She was worried about her children and who would raise them if they were gone running a restaurant.

But it all worked out after a while. My parents did open a restaurant and it became a very successful and prosperous business. My siblings and I all did our part in it and we made enough money for all of us to go to college without getting any financial assistance,

But when they started to get older and the restaurant became too much for them to do alone, I decided to move back home and help out. I was already engaged to Clyde and he was just finishing up law school.

I got married and my husband and I took over the business after both my parents died. I remember when I first told Clyde that I wanted to take over the business. He being this "man of faith" I knew he would first want us to pray over the decision. He prayed about everything. When he made partner at his law firm, before he gave them his answer he came home and prayed. Before he became an Elder at our church he prayed about that. This Negro prayed about everything except our marriage.

During all of his "on-the-knees" praying, he was also on his knees eating every piece of pussy he could find. Clyde had been cheating on me since we met. He was out screwing some woman the night before our wedding. I found out during our reception. He had the nerve to invite the whore to the wedding. When

I asked who she was, he told me that she was the entertainment last night.

I always thought that eventually he would get tired and realize he had a family that was important to him. That's what my father did! When he got tired of cheating on my mother all those years he grew old with her. That's just the way marriage goes.

But in the meantime, in between time, my husband got a hold of some pussy that he couldn't let go of. It was some little young girl half his age.

At first, he had the nerve to bring her to our church where his children and I have been members since the kids were born. But after that first Sunday, the Pastor asked him not to disrespect his wife and children. In other words, he had to leave and find another church home.

Now here I am sitting in my office about to sign some fucking divorce papers. Damn! I just wished I saw all of this coming.

Ring! Ring!

"Hello, this is Amanda."

"Hey Girl, what are you doing?"

"Hey Bobbi what's up? I have been trying to call you for a few days, but I just keep getting your voicemail. Now tell me what's wrong with this picture?"

"Girl I'm sorry. I have been so busy,"

"Busy doing what?"

"Stuff!"

"What kind of stuff?"

"Stuff Amanda. Damn! Why are you messing with me?"

"Stuff like fucking and sucking?"

"Shut-up Amanda! You must've talked to Colleen."

"Of course I have."

"Okay, Darnell and I are back together. Now say what you need say."

"I don't have anything to say Bobbi. Just be careful. And hell, who am I to give advice to anyone on relationships?"

"Did you sign the papers yet?"

"I am about to. I just feel so messed up right now."

"Do you need me to come to the restaurant or meet you at your house?"

"No Bobbi, I'll be fine. I just have to face this and move forward."

"That's right."

"Now I just need to figure out how to do that."

"You know how to do that Amanda. You just have to keep busy."

"You're right Bobbi, but I just think that I am going to need more than that."

"Well you know what they say, the best way to get over a man, is to get under a new one." Bobbi said while laughing.

"You're crazy Bobbi. You know I am not about to bring a man around my kids. They still ask me sometimes if I will let their dad move back in. I know I need to explain things to them, but right now they are just so young."

"Well one day Amanda you are going to have to talk to them about all of this. And anyway, you are not going to always be alone. You are going to meet someone one day and he will want to have a family with you and your kids. You have to believe that."

"Yeah right!"

"It's the truth Amanda. There is someone out there who will love you and your kids forever."

"Do you really believe that Bobbi? Do you really believe that there is a man out there who will be everything I want and need?"

"Yes Amanda I do."

"Well that's funny because my husband was everything I wanted in a man. So what if he cheated, that's just what men do. My father did it all the time."

"Well I don't think this is how love should go. Love is supposed to be true and faithful."

"Do you think you have love with Darnell?"

"I love him. I think he loves me. Well at least that's what he says."

"Do you feel loved by him?"

"You know Amanda, that's the thing. Some times he makes me feel like he can't live without me. And when we are together, I am the most important thing in his world. He shows me so much attention. It reminds me of my father."

"How's that?"

"Well you know that my parents were not a married couple when I was born."

"Yeah."

"But I can remember times when I was young wishing my father would come over and spend time with us. I can remember being so good while he would be at our house wishing this would make him stay."

"Did he ever stay?"

"Sometimes he would be there for two or three days, but never longer."

"I know that had to be hard on you Bobbi. I didn't know it was like that. I am so sorry."

"Girl don't sweat it. I am completely over that and him."

"Do you ever talk to your father?"

"No Amanda, I haven't spoken to him in about twelve years."

"Are you mad at him Bobbi?"

"No not at all. Girl I just figured that that was between him and my mother. That was their love thing. I may never understand it and maybe it's not for me to understand. But I try not to think about it or him most of the time. Anyway, girl let me get off this phone and get to work."

"I know I have to go too. The restaurant is starting to get the lunch crowd in here. I need to go get back out there. See you on Friday, right?"

"For sure! I will call Colleen and confirm with her."

CHAPTER FIVE

Roberta

I didn't call Colleen until I got off work that evening. My day was just so hectic that I just didn't get a chance to call. I had two restaurants to critique and they were an hour and a half away from each other. This was the worst part of the job. Driving all over town and trying to find good parking. Lots of these restaurants are in areas that you have to pay for parking or you will have to walk a country mile to the restaurant. At times like this I really think about finding a new profession. But what other job could I get that would allow me such freedom. I truly only work maybe fifteen to twenty hours a week but I am paid for forty.

When I got home, I didn't see Darnell's car parked outside. He should have been home by now. (I said home, although we don't officially live together yet.)

I walked in my kitchen and threw my keys and purse on the table. I picked up the phone to listen to my messages. I had two messages. One was from my mother and the other one was from Darnell. I picked up my cell phone to see if anyone had tried to call me on it. Just my mother, so I decided to call her back first because she sounded like it was important.

"Hello Mom, how are you doing?"

"Hello Roberta. So you finally got my messages."

"Yes I just walked in the house."

"Well I called you on your cell phone, but you didn't answer that either."

"Sorry Mom. I didn't have my phone on. What's going on?"

"Your father is in the hospital." She said sounding sad.

"He is? What's wrong with him?" I asked very nonchalant.

"He had some type of attack."

"Is he going to be okay? Who's there with him?"

"I guess Marcia and his other kids. You, Dottie and Sherry should go out there."

"You can tell them to go Mom, but I don't really have that kind of time."

"That's the same thing your sisters said. What is wrong with you girls? That man is your father!" She yelled.

My mother is one of those people who thinks you always have to respect your parents no matter what they did to you.

"Mom I am sure he is going to be okay. And anyway, I haven't seen Marshall in twelve years. I wouldn't even know what to say to him. I guess Dottie and Sherry probably feel the same way."

"Well that's what they said. I just wanted you guys to know about your father."

We both were silent for a moment'

"Mom how did you find out that Marshall was in the hospital in the first place?" I asked because I know his wife or kids didn't call her.

"Your Aunt Betty Jean saw his daughter in the emergency room."

"Is Aunt Betty Jean still working in the emergency admittance? Isn't it time for her to retire?"

"Yeah she should have retired five years ago, but she said she's bored and has nothing else to do since all the kids moved out."

"Mom they should have moved out a long time ago. They are both in their mid thirties. None of your kids still live with you."

"I know that's right!" She said and we both started laughing.

"Mom I'll call you later. I really need to finish up some work." I said lying.

"Okay, but don't forget this Friday is Dottie's birthday and you promised to be there."

"Is that this Friday?"

"Yes it is. It's always been the same every year."

I grabbed my blackberry and looked at my calendar. I use my blackberry for everything. My day planner on my phone is where I keep all my appointments and I usually look at it throughout the day. I guess I must have overlooked that date. She was right. It was right there in my face. Dottie's B-day!

"Yes I have it and I'll be there. But I can't stay long because I have to meet Amanda and Colleen."

"You hangout with them all the time, but this week should be about family."

"Mom I said I will be there so I will." I said very firm.

"Good. I will see you then."

"Bye Mom."

"Bye Roberta."

Dang! I forgot all about my sister's party. I really hate going over to my sister's house. My older sister Dorothy, who most people call Dottie, is a very successful banker here in the Twin Cities. She has no children and a husband who is an accountant with a major firm. They live in a huge house right on the lake and every Christmas and any other major holiday, they want everyone to come to their home. The problem with Dottie is that she is so stuck-up that you wouldn't even believe we grew up in the same house.

When Dottie came home from college, she was a completely different person. I guess getting away from our family was what she needed. She was able to meet lots of different people and learn a lot about different cultures. She used to bring different friends home with her and it seemed like every friend she made, she picked up some of their behaviors.

Then there is my baby sister Sherry. She is the one with the children and they are the most lovable kids you ever want to meet. I am very close to my sister's six year old twin boys. Sherry has a live in boyfriend who is hard working and loves his boys to death. She works as a teacher and is finishing up a Master's degree in special education. Her boyfriend Riley works in construction. He really wants to marry Sherry, but she keeps saying that she likes things the way they are. She gets that shit from our mother. She thinks it is okay not to be married to your kid's father.

I decided to cook dinner and wait on Darnell to get home. I cooked steak and potatoes and made a toss salad. His message said he was going to be a few hours late. He was going to stop by his parent's house before he made it back to me. I forgot to give Colleen a call. I wonder what she's up to. She was probably dealing with that monster daughter of hers. Sometimes I wonder why Colleen just won't pop her upside her head. But what do I know. I don't have any kids yet.

Colleen

"Sabrina I got your grades today and I am so upset with you."

"Why? I already told you last week that I didn't do that well this quarter." Sabrina said while walking up the stairs.

"Sabrina, do not walk away from me while I'm talking. Get your little ass back down here."

"Why, I thought you were finished." She shouted from the top of the stairs.

"Do you still see me standing here?"

"Yes."

"Then bring yourself back down here and sit until I'm finished."

She stomped back down the spiral staircase.

"What else do you want me to say Mom? I didn't do my best, but I'm sure next quarter will be better." She said with no emotion.

"Are you just giving up Sabrina? Because it seems like you just don't care anymore."

"I care Mom. I just got a lot on my mind right now." She said still with no emotion.

We both were quiet for a second until I decided to break the ice.

"I am really starting to worry about you Sabrina. You don't talk to me anymore and you are always angry. Is this about your father?"

She blew her breath and turned her head.

"Sabrina I can't help you if you don't talk to me. I love you so please let me help you."

"Mom I don't need any help. I am fine."

"Is this about a boy Sabrina?"

"No, this is not about a boy Mom. It's not about anything or anybody. I just need to get upstairs and start on my homework."

More silence.

"One more thing Sabrina, I just want you to know that you are the most important person in my life. I just think since your father's death you have been so distant. This is a time for us to reach out to each other. I want you to know if you ever need to talk, I am here for you."

"I know that Mom. You have always been here for me."

"Sabrina, what if I take some time off and we take a little vacation just the two of us. How does that sound?"

"What about school?" She asked.

"You can make up the work or take it with you."

"If I take my school work with me, then it won't be much of a vacation."

"Well you have a point. What about around the Memorial Day holiday?"

"I don't know Mom. Let's play it by ear."

"Okay Sabrina, that's fine."

"Can I go up to my room now?"

"Go ahead Sabrina."

She got up and walked out of the living room and up the stairs. She didn't even look back to see if I was still looking at her. What am I going to do? I can't just sit back and do nothing. Maybe I could get her some help. Maybe what she really needs is to talk to someone about her father's death and what she is going through. He may have been an ass to me, but he loved Sabrina and never beat her.

Ring!

"Hello."

"Hey Colleen, what are you guys doing?"

"Hey Bobbi, we are just finishing up dinner."

"Why are you guys eating so late?"

"We've been out and about all evening and didn't grab anything to eat. I don't know why I'm cooking though. Sabrina will probably not even come down to eat."

"Are you guys having problems again?"

"Girl yes we are. I don't know what else to do. It's like I can't reach her. Bobbi I am getting so scared that I might lose her."

"Colleen, don't say stuff like that. You are not going to lose Sabrina. She's a teenager and she's probably going through some teenage shit."

"That's what I thought at first Bobbi. But she keeps assuring me that nothing is going on. I am thinking about taking her on a trip during Memorial Day. Maybe if we get away from here then we could do some mother and daughter bonding."

"Where are you thinking about going?"

"I was thinking maybe to the Bahamas or somewhere in the US Virgin Islands."

"Both of those places sound amazing! She will love that!"

"I hope so Bobbi. I don't want anything to push us further and further apart."

"It'll be fine Colleen. Just keep the faith."

"I will try girl. Well enough of that, will I see you on Friday?"

"Yes, but I'll be late. It's my sister Dottie's birthday and I promised my mother that I'll stop by."

"I know you hate that."

"Girl, you wouldn't believe it."

"Believe me I know. I can hardly take an hour with my family."

"Tell me about it. Look, I will let you get back to cooking dinner Colleen. Call me if you need to talk later."

"Thanks Bobbi, I will see you on Friday."

"Bye Girl."

CHAPTER SIX

Amanda

I am so glad it's Friday. I have really been looking forward to seeing my girls and telling them about the crazy week I've had. The restaurant has been jumping and business has never been better, so I really can't complain about that at all. But I am so busy with the kids and the house, that I just don't have enough hours in the day. The one thing that makes it all worthwhile is the fact that I will be hanging with my girls and all will be fine.

We have barely talked much this week, so they don't even know about the handsome gentleman that has been frequenting my restaurant all week. At first I thought that he was the competition, but then I found out that he is a friend of Joe's. He's in town doing some real estate work. I think he buys and sells houses. (At least that's what I understand.)

He first came in for lunch at the beginning of the week and I noticed him as soon as I walked out of the kitchen. He looked so professional. He had on black slacks, a black turtleneck crop top, and a brown tweed blazer. His hair is salt and pepper and so is his beard and mustache. He seemed to be older than he looked, but there was just something about him. I have never seen a man so put together. He just looked like he had class.

Joe was sitting at the table with him when I walked out. He waved for me to join them. My goodness! I didn't even have on any lipstick. I walked over to say hello. They both stood up when I approached the table. I could tell he was an inch taller than I was and I had on high heels. The good looking man reached for my hand.

"Amanda this is my good friend Hamilton Laws. Hamilton this is my boss and good friend Amanda Walker." Joe did the introductions.

We shook hands. His hands were so soft.

"Hello Amanda. I am very pleased to meet you."

"Hello Hamilton I am pleased to meet you too." I said. "Please sit down and finish your meal."

"Only if you'll join us?"

"Oh no, I couldn't. I have so much work to finish in the kitchen. I don't have time for lunch." I said trying not to look in his face. But damn! There was something about this man. Oh my God he is too fine.

"I know you can take a break for a couple of minutes can't you?"

"No, you guys enjoy your lunch. I really didn't mean to intrude."

"Please join us or have coffee with us." He said sounding like he was begging. Joe just sat there with this stupid grin on his face.

"Okay, I can do coffee. But just as long as I am not intruding on your lunch?"

"You are not intruding. We were actually just finishing up." Joe said.

"Okay I can do coffee. But first let me check on some things in the kitchen and I'll be right back."

"That sounds great!" Hamilton said.

I walked away and headed back in the kitchen. I couldn't help smiling as I entered. My head Chef was looking in my direction. He smiled at me as if he knew why I was smiling.

When I walked back out into the restaurant Hamilton was at the table alone. I think Joe set me up. This is a good set up though. I walked over to the table and he stood up again.

"Oh please sit down." I said.

We both sat down.

"I am so glad you were able to join me for coffee Amanda."

"I am really glad too. I don't get a chance to sit for coffee too often."

One of my waitresses came over with a pot of coffee. She poured us both a cup. She was also smiling when she looked at me.

"Thank you Amy." I said.

"You are very welcome Ms. Walker." She said and walked away.

"Amanda, Joe tells me that you own this restaurant."

"Yes I do. My parents owned it first and then when they were not able to run it anymore my ex-husband and I took it over."

"Well it is a beautiful place. I don't think that I have ever seen a soul food restaurant this nice before."

"Thank you. I wanted to make it as upscale as possible, but yet still have that down home appeal."

"Oh you captured that." He said looking around.

"Thank you Hamilton." I said and took a sip of my coffee. I was trying desperately not to stare at this man. He has to be at least fifteen years older than I, but he still looked good enough to nibble on.

"So Amanda, what is there to do in this town? I am here for the week and I would like to find a place to relax and maybe listen to a little jazz."

"Well I don't know if Joe told you or not, but I have a nice jazz band here on the weekends. They're really good. You should stop by. I'm surprised Joe didn't mention it to you."

"Well actually he did. I just wanted you to invite me." He said and flashed this smile that could melt the hardest heart. I smiled back.

"Tell me Hamilton, what brings you to the twin cities?"

"I am looking to buy some property here that I can fix up and resale."

"That sounds interesting. So is this the only place you're looking or does your business take you to many different cities?"

"Well right now I do travel a lot. I don't see a need to stay at home."

"Why not, don't you have a family?"

"My wife died some years ago and my children are all grown now."

"Oh I am sorry about your wife Hamilton. I didn't mean to pry."

"No need to apologize Amanda. Actually my wife passed away at a young age. I raised my boys alone and they are both doing quite well for themselves."

"What do they do for a living?"

"One is a Marine and the other is an Attorney. They both have beautiful wives and wonderful kids."

"Wow! They are doing well. I just hope my children end up doing as well. I am a single parent also."

"I'm sure they will."

"How can you be so sure?"

"Well with a mother like you, how can they not do well?"

"Thanks, but you don't even know me. We just met and have only had coffee."

"There's just something about you. I could tell you were a good person when you walked out of the kitchen. I have that gift."

"You can tell all that just by watching me walk?"

"Not just your walk, but also your presence."

"That is very kind of you Hamilton, but now it's time for me to get back to work. It was very nice meeting you." I said and stood up to leave. He stood up too.

"Have dinner with me tonight Amanda."

"I can't. I have to get home to my kids and deal with homework, dinner, and any other dramas that we single parents have to deal with."

"Get a sitter. I would just like to get to know you better that's all. I am only in town for a short time, but I would love to spend some of that time with you if that's possible?"

"I don't know Hamilton. I really need to think about it."

"Don't think about it, just say yes. Here's my cell number and the number to my hotel. Just call me and tell me where to pick you up."

"Maybe I could meet you somewhere."

"That's fine too. Just let me know where."

"I'll do that. Talk to you later." I said.

"I'll be looking forward to it Amanda." He said as I walked away.

I smiled.

That was the beginning of the week. We have been hanging out ever since and he's had lunch here at the restaurant every day this week. He is leaving this weekend, so we have been making the most of our time together. We haven't had sex or anything like that but he sure can kiss. I never imagined in a million years that someone much older than I could be so much fun and so fucking sexy. I can't wait to tell the girls. They are going to trip! I am so glad its Friday!

Roberta

I am so glad that it's Friday. Not because I get to go to my sister's party, but it is the only time I have with Colleen and Amanda at the same time. I have two sisters, but these two are my real sisters. We keep it real! I need to tell them how tired I am of Darnell's black ass. He is up to his old tricks again. Staying out late and lying about what time he'll be over. I swear I don't know why I put up with him. He is never going to be a man of his word. I guess I hold on waiting on that one day when he will say to me, "Baby I'm here to stay!"

This week has been hard though. My mother keeps calling me about going to the hospital to see my dad. But I am just not feeling that.

Now here I am driving to the other part of town to a party that I don't even want to go to. Darnell promised he would go with me, but as always he didn't show up. I had to leave so I could make an appearance, play with my nephews and get to Amanda's place for my "real" good time.

I pulled up in her circle driveway and all I could think about was how fake my sister Dottie is. I know tonight she is going to really put on airs.

"Hey girl, I am so happy that you made it!" Dottie said as soon as she opened the door.

"Of course I would make it. It's not every day your older sister turns forty." I said as we hugged.

"Okay smart ass! You know I am only thirty-nine today."

"Is that the lie you're telling everyone or just me?"

We hugged again as we laughed.

"Here you go Dottie." I said as I handed her a gift.

"Is this a present for me?"

"Don't be fake big sis! You know if I would have showed up empty handed, I would have been the talk of the family."

"You know that's right! Come in, everyone is in the family room. Food and drinks are in there also."

Her family room is huge. And all of the family was in there. My mother was sitting on a couch, my sister Sherry and her family was eating at a table, a couple of aunts and uncles were dancing, and a few cousins that I haven't seen in decades were making their way to the bar. Dottic is terrible. She only invited all of the family here to see her house. Mark my word, after tonight, this is the one and only time that they will get an invite back to her house.

"Come her baby and give your mother a huge."

"Hey Mom, how did you get here? I called you to see if you needed a ride."

"Dottie sent Richard to pick me up."

"That was nice of them."

"It sure was. He picked me up in the new car he just bought for Dottie."

"Really, what kind of car is it?"

"It is a Lexus. And it is the nicest car that I have ever been in."

Everyone knows that Dottie probably bought that car herself. She is the one who makes all the money, but she loves to make people think that her husband buys her these expensive things. However I know the truth.

"I'm not saying that your car isn't nice too dear."

"I know Mom."

"What kind of car is that again?"

"I drive a BMW Mom."

"Oh yeah, they call that the Black-Man-Wish car. But I don't know why. I guess because it's so expensive. Only single people with good jobs can afford it."

"I guess so. I need a drink. Will you excuse me Mom for a minute?"

"Yes Dear, but come right back. I want you to hear what your Aunt Betty Jean said about your father."

I walked away fast. Sometimes I just can't take much of my mother. I promise I am going to have a drink then I am out of here.

"Hey Sis I am so glad you made it."

"Hey Sherry, how long have you been here?"

"Long enough, I think I am going to give it another hour or so and I am out."

"I'm not even giving it an hour."

"I saw you over there talking to Mom. Was she mentioning Marshall to you?"

"Yes she was. Sometimes I don't get her. Why does she so desperately want us to acknowledge this man as our father? He never really acknowledged us."

"I know Bobbi. It's as if she has forgotten all the times that we needed him and he never showed up."

"I don't know if she forgot or if it even bothered her."

"Hell, it didn't bother me until I got older and realized that real fathers were not part time. They don't just pop-up once or twice a month."

"That's not part-time Sherry, that's seasonal."

We both laughed. Although it was nothing to laugh at, because that was our father we were speaking of.

I had a few drinks more than I planned and said my good-byes. It was so many people there that I knew I could slip out without anyone noticing. I was so happy to get out of there. It was as if I had just been freed from prison.

All the way to Amanda's restaurant I could only think of my mother. I don't know why, but she was really getting on my nerves this evening. I really need to sit her down and talk to her about this whole Marshall thing. What is her motivation behind this? I am going to tell her the truth. Marshall was a sorry father to us. Me, personally, I don't want to have anything to do with him or anyone like him. (Or do I?) Whatever, I am so glad it's Friday!

Colleen

I am glad it's Friday. I get to hang with my girls and tell them about the insane week that I have had.

Work is finally going great. Finally, I am not so worried about some young anchor woman taking my AM spot. My contract is good and I am pleased with it. For once, Colleen Dubois feels good about herself and her job.

My home is another story. Sabrina seems to be drifting further and further away. Sometimes she acts like she is on drugs or something. I searched her room the other day and found nothing. I took her to get a physical last week, and I asked the doctor to test her urine and blood for any type of drugs. I got the results today and she is clean. So I don't know what else to do.

This weekend she is spending some time with my brother's family. I hope it goes great. She has not been with her cousin since years before her father's death. She and Novi used to be so close when they were younger. They are around the same age (only months separate them) and have somewhat of the same demeanor. They both are the only child in their families and a little spoiled.

"Hurry up Sabrina. Your Uncle Edward will be here in a minute."

"I'm coming Mom. I'm just getting some CDs to take with me."

"Girl, get down these stairs. I am sure Novi has the same music you have. You are both the same age remember."

"I wish you wouldn't yell at me from down here Mom. I can here you just fine. Your voice carries." She said smiling as she walked down the stairs.

"Well don't make me yell and don't laugh at me." I said. (I really didn't mind. It was so nice to see her smile again.)

"Hey that's the door Sabrina! They're here!"

"I'll get it Mom!"

"Thanks dear."

"Hello Uncle Edward!"

"Hey Baby!" My brother said while hugging Sabrina.

"Hey Novi!"

"Hey Bri, I missed you so much!" Novi said and they hugged for what seemed like forever.

I hugged my brother and my niece too. I realized I missed my brother so much, but he stopped coming around after he found out about the abuse. He wanted me to leave but I wouldn't. He used to get so mad at me and say that I was putting Sabrina through the same thing our parents put us through.

I remember when my brother Edward first found out about the abuse. Sabrina was probably three years old then. (I had been living with the abuse for about five years by then.) We were all at his house for a birthday party for him when he and his wife noticed a bruise on my arm. Edward hit the roof! He grabbed my husband and beat the shit out of him. They ruined the whole party. Everyone was yelling and the kids were crying. It was terrible. I ended up staying with my brother for about four days. Then I went home.

Through the years we went back and forth. I would leave and then go back. This made my whole family angry. After a while, I just stayed away from everyone. I even kept Sabrina away. And now that Morris is dead, I decided that it was time for Sabrina to be around her family again. And my brother totally agreed.

"You guys come in. Have a seat."

"Damn little Sis, you have done some amazing things with this house." Edward said while looking around.

"Yeah, it's a little different then when you last saw it." I said.

"Come on upstairs Novi so I can show you my room."

"Great!"

"Now you girls hurry back down. I am sure Edward has some things he needs to do besides wait on you two to come back down here."

"No, really I'm fine. Lois is working late so I am going to take the girls out to dinner and hang with them for a while. Or until they get tired of me."

"Which probably won't be too much longer, you don't really believe that teenage girls want to spend a Friday night with us old folks?"

"Why not? I can be a lot of fun."

"Whatever!" I said and started laughing. It was so good to be sitting talking to my brother without worrying about any drama. That hasn't happened in so long.

"So what do you have planned for the evening?" Edward asked.

"I am going to do the same thing that I do every Friday night. I am going to meet my girls at the restaurant that Amanda owns and have a nice night."

"Oh yeah, I remember your friends from the funeral. They seem like really nice girls. And they are so pretty too."

"Yeah, we beautiful women tend to stick together." I said smiling.

"Whatever!"

We sat and talked for a few minutes longer before the girls came back down. It felt like old times.

"Well are you ladies ready?" Edward asked and stood up.

"Yes we are." They both said at the same time.

"Alright, let's roll."

"Be on your best behavior Sabrina."

"Mom, I'm always on my best behavior."

"Alright, give me a hug and call me later."

"I will Mom." She said.

I hugged Sabrina and then Novi. When I hugged my brother Edward, it was like we didn't want to let each other go. He didn't even hug me this hard at the funeral.

"It is good seeing you Sis."

"It is great seeing you too. Let's never let this happen to us again. It has been too long." I said.

"I agree." He said sounding all choked up.

They left and I shut the door behind them. I needed to hurry and change clothes and get to the restaurant. I know the girls are waiting for me. I'm so glad it is Friday.

CHAPTER SEVEN

Roberta

Last night was great! It was so good hanging with Amanda and Colleen last night. We ended up hanging out until after midnight. We hardly ever stay out that late, but we were having so much fun. Amanda's new friend even joined us for a while. He is so nice and so handsome. I think he really likes her and it seems she likes him too. They are planning on spending the whole day together today. I think they make a nice couple. Amanda must think so too because she never takes a day off.

It was also good to hear that Colleen and her brother are working on their relationship. I know she misses him a lot. She sacrificed a lot to be with that terrible husband of hers. Now that he's gone maybe they can move on with their lives and leave the past behind. I don't always get along with my sisters, but I would hate if I didn't talk to them for long periods of time.

I told them last night that Darnell is officially out of my life. I can't take his shit anymore. Lately he has been up to his old tricks. He's with me sometimes and then he's gone. He's always promising me that things are going to get better. But the difference this time, I am not saying much about his lies and his disappearing acts to him. Why bother? He's just going to tell me what he thinks I want to hear. I think I have become immune to his stories. Like now, he's on his way here. (He says.) When he gets here, I am going to sit him down and tell him that it is over and that I AM MOVING ON!

"Baby that was the best sex I have ever had! Girl I swear you must be magic."

"Shut up Darnell! You're just saying that."

"Roberta I am serious. Girl you don't know how good it feels to be laying here on a Saturday afternoon in your arms."

"It is nice Darnell, but I have to get up and get to the hair salon."

"No not now baby. I just got here and I missed you so much. This week has been so crazy. I just want to hold you in my arms. So please, let's just lay here in bed for the whole day." He said and put his arms around me.

"Darnell I can't lay here all day. I have to get to the salon. My hair is a mess and staying here in this bed is not going to help my perm much." I said rubbing my head.

"Baby your hair is fine. Please don't leave me."

"Stop playing man! I will be back in a couple of hours. Will you still be here when I get back?"

"Yeah, I'll be here. I'll just stay here and watch some television."

"Good! I'm going to take a shower." I said and got up.

"Wait, I'm coming too!"

I don't know what just happened. My every intention was to say goodbye to Darnell but the moment he walked in my place, I took one look at him and he made me melt. He started kissing me on my neck and then the next thing I know, we were in the bed fucking like two animals. I swear this man is the one who is magic. He does the most annoying things, but then I see him and he touches me and that's all she wrote. I melt.

"Girl I am so sorry that I'm late. Traffic was terrible."

"That's okay Bobbi. My last customer never showed up so you're straight."

"Thanks Tammy you are the bomb."

"Come on back to the sink." She said. I followed behind her.

"Girl it's crowded in here today. Is everyone going out tonight?" I asked.

"Naw, its Saturday. People just want to look good for church tomorrow."

"You're crazy! I just want to look good for tonight."

"You got plans tonight Bobbi?"

"No not really. I just have a man at home waiting on me. I just want to look good for him."

"You will. Put your head back so I can wash this hair and make you beautiful."

"Are you sure that I don't need a perm?"

"Girl your hair is fine. Trust me."

It took Tammy two hours to finish me up. That's because her missing customer showed up and she was doing both of our heads at the same time. I didn't mind though. I knew when she finished I would look like a new woman. I was right.

"Here you go." She said and handed me a mirror.

"Tammy, girl you know you can work miracles. My hair was a mess!"

"Bobbi you always say that and your hair is never that bad."

"It was today. But you can't tell by looking at me now." I said handing her a fifty dollar bill.

"Thanks Bobbi! I really appreciate you."

"No, I really appreciate you. What did you say you were doing this evening?"

"I am going to this white party."

"Will there be any blacks there?" I asked joking with her.

"Of course Bobbi there will be. You're trying to be funny!"

"I just thought because you're white, it was a party for just your people." I said laughing.

"It's not for white people, it's a party where everyone wears white smart ass!"

"I know girl, I'm just fucking with you. As long as you keep laying my hair out like this we will always be sisters, even if you are a shade or two lighter." We gave each other a high five and started laughing.

"So tell me about this party."

"Well you know that I am a part of this women's group called the Queen's Project."

"What's the Queen's Project? You never told me about this group."

"Yes I did Bobbi. Remember you asked if it was some man bashing group."

"Oh yeah, now I remember!"

"I also remember that you said that you would come with me one day. Tonight is our annual party where we invite different people to speak and talk about when they first learned they were Queens. We party afterwards and just have a good time."

"Is there any guys at the party?"

"Yes, tonight we can bring anyone we like as long as they have on white. Why do you want to come?"

"No, girl I'm straight. I told you I have to get home to my man."

"Does he treat you like a Queen?"

"I don't know how a Queen is to be treated."

"Then maybe you should come to one of our meetings."

"Maybe I will one day. I will let you know."

"You have been telling me that forever."

"Well then you must believe me, because I keep saying the same thing and you know I wouldn't lie to you."

"Yes I know. So I will just wait until you decide that today is the day that you join me."

"I will surprise you."

"It will be a surprise if you come. But believe me it will be a welcomed surprised."

I left the salon and headed home but all I kept thinking about was Tammy's question. *Does he treat you like a Queen*? Hell no he doesn't! He does make me feel good when we are together and making mad passionate love. But is that enough? Is that enough for me and any other woman? How do I know for sure?

I kept looking in the mirror at myself. I must admit it, I looked good! I can't wait until I get home so Darnell can see me. Who am I kidding? I know he is not still at my place waiting on me. That's why I waited around the salon shooting the shit with Tammy. If I really was trying to get home to my man, I would have hurried my ass out of there as soon as she was finished with my hair.

When I pulled into my complex to my surprise Darnell's car was still where it was when I left. I am shocked.

I walked in and I could smell food cooking. He had cooked baked chicken with a mushroom sauce, steamed veggies, and baked potatoes. I was surprised to say the least.

We had a good night! By the next morning you couldn't even tell I had even been to the hair salon the day before.

CHAPTER EIGHT

Amanda

I must be dreaming. Somebody pinch me. This man can't be real! He is too perfect. Hamilton and I have been spending every day together. He is leaving today, but I understand. I know he has to get back to his job like I have to do mine. I have to admit it though; it is good to take time off from work for you sometimes. I should do this more often with or without a man. I have a very capable manager. Joe can run the place with his eyes closed. He can run the restaurant in my absence and he is also the bartender on the weekends. I trust him completely and I should take advantage of this more often.

"Hello, this is Amanda."

"Hello beautiful."

"Hello Hamilton, I was just thinking about you."

"Good thoughts I hope."

"Nothing but."

"Tell me what you were thinking." He said.

"I was thinking about what a wonderful time I have been having with you. It has been a pleasure meeting you."

"You act like we will never see each other again."

"No, I'm not saying that. I'm just saying that I know how it is."

"How what is Amanda? I'm confused."

"You know what I'm saying Hamilton."

"No I don't dear. Explain it to me."

"Hamilton, I know how business men who travel a lot are. I know that you go to different cities all the time."

"Yes I do. But what does that mean?"

"It means that I understand that I am just someone you met in this city and had fun with. Don't get me wrong Hamilton, I had fun too!"

He started laughing.

"Why are you laughing? We did have a good time right?"

"Amanda I had a great time. And I thought this was more than just a chance meeting. I thought we both felt something. Am I mistaken?"

"No Hamilton, you're not mistaken. I am just saying I understand if this is goodbye."

"Amanda, when you left my hotel room this morning did I say goodbye?"

"No you didn't."

"What did I say baby?"

"You said you would see me later."

"What else did I say when I kissed you?"

"You said this feels right."

"Yes I did. And I meant that. I wasn't just talking about the love making, I was talking about everything."

We both were quiet. I didn't know what to say.

"Baby you still there?"

"Yes Hamilton, I'm still here."

"Damn!"

"What's wrong?"

"Do you know how good that sounds? I would love for it to always be like that."

"Like what?"

"I want to go take care of business with work and pick up a phone and always here you say that."

"Say what?"

"I'm still here."

I smiled as a tear ran down my face. This is the sweetest man I have ever met and he is leaving today.

"Well I know you probably have a lot of packing to do, so I better let you get to it. I wouldn't want you to miss your flight. (Yes I would.)

"Okay, I have about an hour before I have to get out of here."

"Call me when you get home."

"You know I will. Amanda, I hope you know that I will be back soon."

"I hope so. I would love to see you again Hamilton."

"Baby you will see me soon. I'll call when I get in."

"Ok Hamilton and have a save flight."

"I will and I will call you later today."

We hung up the phone and the tears wouldn't stop running down my face. How could this be happening? How have I let myself fall so quick? I feel like a teenager. Women my age don't get caught up so easily. I feel so silly. I need to call my girls.

"Hello Bobbi, can you call Colleen on the three-way."

"What's wrong Amanda? Is everything okay?"

"I just need to talk to both of my girls right now."

"Hold on and let me go in the other room."

She put me on hold.

"Hello."

"Colleen it's us."

"Three-way calling, this must be serious!"

"It is! I am so sad."

"What happened Amanda?" Colleen asked.

"Hamilton is leaving today and I am so sad."

"Oh Amanda, I am so sorry. Do you want us to come over?"

"No Bobbi I will be okay. It's just that I am going to miss him."

"I know Amanda, but why are you acting like you won't see him again?

"Colleen you know how it is."

"No Amanda I don't."

"Yeah I want to know too Amanda."

"Ladies, now you both know that men like Hamilton probably go from town to town picking up women like me."

"What the fuck are you talking about Amanda? What do you mean women like you?" Bobbi yelled.

"Bobbi you know what I mean."

"No I don't Amanda. Please tell me."

"Yes Amanda, please tell me too." Colleen said.

"I'm talking about men who travel most of time. They probably meet women on the road, tell them sweet things, and treat them like Queens. They hit it and then leave."

"Amanda you sound crazy."

"Colleen I'm serious."

"Did he hit it right though?" Bobbi asked.

"Bobbi is that all you think about?"

"Yes Amanda, as a matter of fact that is all I think about. And please don't tell me that you don't think about dick."

"No I believe that good dick is only as good as the man it is connected to."

"Bullshit Amanda! I have had some great sexual encounters with men who I could not stand. They just had that magic stick."

"I have to agree with Amanda Bobbi. You have to have a connection with a man for the love making to be great."

"You two don't know shit about dick. Both of you heifers have only had two lovers a piece so that doesn't count."

We all started laughing.

"But seriously Amanda, you act as if you were just a booty-call. Do you feel like that?"

"No Colleen, that's not what I'm saying."

"Then what are you saying Amanda?"

"I'm just saying maybe I fell for the oldest trick in the book."

"You know damn well you didn't fall for any trick. You just fell for a man girl!"

"Bobbi I am not saying that I fell for him at all."

"Oh yeah my dear, you fell. Or why else would you be sad?" Colleen said.

"Okay I like the man! Is that what ya'll bitches wanted me to say?"

"Yes Amanda, just admit it. You have fallen in love with Hamilton."

"Colleen I am not in love with Hamilton. I just like him a lot."

"Bullshit! You are in love Amanda. Just admit it."

"Bobbi you are crazy! Both of you guys are crazy!"

"Yeah and you're crazy in love."

"No I'm not Colleen."

"What's the problem with admitting you love someone Amanda?"

"There's no problem Bobbi, it's just how could I love someone so soon?"

"Love doesn't have a time limit Amanda. Love just shows up when you least expect it."

"I know that Colleen, remember I did have a husband once."

"We are not talking about your marriage Amanda. We're talking about true love."

"I had true love Colleen."

"You had a marriage just like I had."

"Anyway, I just want to say that he must have really put it on your tired ass!"

"Okay Bobbi, I admit it. He made love to me like I never had it before. I mean Clyde was a good lover, but Hamilton knows how to make love."

"I knew it! You are whipped!"

"Okay Bobbi, if that is what you want to call it then I'm it! Ladies thank you and I will see you both on Friday."

We all hung up at the same time.

CHAPTER NINE

Colleen

I can't believe how good this week has been at work and at home. Sabrina is spending more time at my brother's house and we are talking a lot more too. It seems she woke up when my brother and his family started coming back around. Maybe that's what she needed. Maybe living out here away from family and dealing with the sudden death of her father was too much for her.

Last weekend we went to dinner at my brother's house, and Sabrina and her cousin Novi were the life of the party. They were so crazy! We thought they would never stop talking and laughing. It was great to see them having so much fun together again. It is also so nice for me to have my brother and sister-in-law in my life again. I missed them so much. I never realized how much I let that "no good" husband of mine steal so much from me. He robbed me of my family relationships, my relationships with my friends, and most important the relationship with my daughter. I am sorry he died, but sometimes I'm glad he's gone.

I am so glad it's the weekend. We had such a good time last night at Amanda's restaurant. I know she felt better by the end of the night. She was really sad at first about Hamilton leaving, but Bobbi and I soon cheered her up. Also, she felt better anyway because Hamilton called and said he wanted her to come visit him next week. I really hope she decides to go. But knowing Amanda, she is going to make-up every excuse in the book not to go. If it was me, I would leave the kids with their dad, and let my manager run the restaurant and be out. Man I wish I could meet a nice guy! But maybe it's too early to bring a man around Sabrina. Speaking of Sabrina, I need to get her up so we can go pick up Bobbi and do some shopping.

Roberta

I am moving slow this morning. I know Colleen and Sabrina will be here in a few minutes. Last night at Amanda's, I told Colleen that I wanted to go shopping with them today. Colleen always finds good sales and I am looking forward to seeing Sabrina. Colleen says she is doing so much better lately. That was so good to hear.

Darnell has been sticking to me lately like white on rice. I am not saying he changed, but lately he has been here with me four to five times a week. It's nice but scary. I just keep thinking that he is going to go back to his old ways. Maybe this time will be different. I learned if I don't nag him then we get along just great. He's just one of those men who can't take a woman nagging him. Sort of like my father

Marshall. My mother had that kind of relationship with him. They got along good as long as she wasn't bugging him about when he was coming over or when he would be back. Oh my God! Darnell is acting like Marshall. I know I must be crazy now. I always told myself that I never wanted to be bothered with a man that I have to wait around for. My mother did this for so long. Hell, sometimes I still think that she is waiting on Marshall to leave his wife and be with her. She used to date other men, but I haven't seen any man at my mom's house in over fifteen years. Sometimes I wish she could meet someone and have a relationship, but she has to get out more to do that. All my mother ever does now since she retired is go to church and sometimes hang with my aunt at her house. My mother is still a beautiful woman and could get a man if she truly wanted one.

I remember this one man that she met at church that seemed pretty nice at first, but she said he was too set in his ways. He didn't want to go out to restaurants and he only wanted to watch TV and hang around the house. I don't know why she was complaining about that because that's all she does anyway. Sometimes I feel sorry for her and maybe she feels sorry for me too.

Amanda

Last night was great! I'm not talking about hanging with my girls, (although that was great too), but I am talking about Hamilton. He called yesterday before I met with the girls and we talked for over two hours. It was wonderful hearing his voice and hearing him say that he missed me and wants me to come there. I said yes and I can't wait to leave. He wants to send me a ticket to leave in two weeks. That's kind of soon, but so what! I am out of here! I don't remember the last time I went anywhere without my kids, but believe me I am going to enjoy every minute of this trip.

I just have to call their father and let him know when I'm leaving and how long I'll be gone. He won't mind though. He spends a lot of time with all his kids. Mine and the one he has with his new girlfriend. He was a cheating no-good husband, but he doesn't cheat his kids. He's always been a good father. But wait, does a good father destroy his family by always creeping around with other women. My father did it all the time, but he never left us. He was there for everything that went on in our lives. I don't even remember my mother ever complaining about him not being home or being gone too long. But it was a different time then and women were a different breed also.

My mother was a strong woman who never complained about anything. My father was demanding and he was somewhat of a chauvinist. He never beat my mother or anything like that, but he wanted everyone to know that he was the man in the relationship and what he said was the bottom line. My mother agreed with most of the decisions he made but when he was wrong she would let him know in a very polite way.

I can remember this one time when my father decided to have a huge party at the house for all of his drunken cousins and some of their whores. My mother put her foot down as soon as she walked in the house and saw all of those people sitting in there. She had just got home from working at the restaurant all day and was tired as hell. She must have seen all those cars parked in the driveway and lost her mind. She walked in the house and gave my father this look, and immediately he told everyone to get their shit and go. She didn't say one word but he knew exactly what she was thinking.

My ex-husband never cared about what I was thinking. When he finally met a women that he wanted to leave me for, he didn't care about the look on my face, or how he looked in front of his children. I was hurt, but looking back that was the best thing that could have happened to us. He was never going to be faithful to me and I was never going to complain about it. I just thought that relationships go through things and that is what makes them strong in the end. Boy was I wrong!

CHAPTER TEN

Amanda

My plane left at 10:00 AM and I was in Atlanta by that afternoon. I was so nervous, although Hamilton had tried desperately to make me feel relaxed over the past two weeks about coming to visit him there. I told him that I would call him as soon as I arrive and get my luggage.

Arriving at the airport was an adventure. I had to catch a train to baggage claim which was something that I had never had to do before. This airport was huge with so many different people. I finally made it to the baggage claim and decided to give Hamilton a call to let him know that I was here.

"Hello Hamilton. I am here."

"Great! I can't wait to see you! Where are you?"

"I am standing in the baggage claim area."

"Where, I don't see you."

"I don't see you either. Where are you Hamilton?"

"Turn around beautiful."

"Hamilton!"

"Give me a hug baby! I missed you so much!"

"I missed you too!" I said while hugging him.

"Damn that feels so good."

"You do too Hamilton."

"Here, let me get your bags so we can get out of here."

"Cool."

We left the airport and drove about forty-five minutes before we made it to his house. He held my hand all the way while he drove. He asked if I was hungry and if I needed anything. He is so considerate.

"No I ate something before I left."

"That was almost three hours ago."

"I'm fine Hamilton. I'll eat later." I said.

We rode and made small talk about his city and about how nice the weather is in Atlanta. I couldn't believe that anyone would ever want to leave this place. Everything looked so nice and so peaceful. The streets were nice and the neighborhood that we pulled into was very upscale. I knew Hamilton was doing well, but this neighborhood looked like he was a rich man. I guess business must be good because this has to be the biggest house that I have ever seen up close and personal.

"Well here we are."

"This is your house?"

"Yes, is something wrong baby?"

"Nothing is wrong Hamilton. Wow this is a mansion!"

He started laughing, but I was so serious. I've never seen a house this big. I can't wait to see the inside of this puppy!

"This is not a mansion dear, but it is a big house."

"I know you said you had a huge house, but I never expected this!"

"I told you baby I need space."

"This is a lot of space Hamilton. How many bedrooms do you have?"

"I have five bedrooms and six bathrooms."

"Tell me what does a single man need with all this space?"

"Well at first it was great when the boys were still home and when my mother was still alive.

"Your mom lived with you?"

"Yes she lived here from the time my wife died and then until her death five years ago."

"So she helped you with the boys?"

"Yes she did. And I thank God for that. My mother was here with the boys while I traveled and built my business."

"That's a good mother."

"Yes she was. I miss her a lot."

"Tell me about it. I miss my parents every day."

"So come on in and let me show you around."

When I walked in I couldn't believe my eyes. He had incredible taste. Everything was so elegant and it looked like his place was a model home. You know those model homes that you visit when you are looking to buy a house. That is exactly what his house looked like.

He showed me around his beautiful house and every room was clean and smelt good. It was not what I expected though. I thought his house would have "man" stuff thrown all over the place. But instead it looked like he barely lived here. Each room was decorated as if he had someone come in and do it for him. Maybe he did. I just can't see him doing all this by himself.

"Did you decorate all of this by yourself?"

"No not at all! I hired an interior decorator when I remolded the house a few years ago."

"Well it is beautiful."

"Thank you dear. I am glad you like it."

"I love it!"

We spent the evening talking and looking at family portraits. His sons are so handsome. They look a lot like he does. He also showed me pictures of their mother. She was a very nice looking young lady. She died too soon he said. I believe she was the love of his life. I didn't mind him showing me her pictures either. I once thought I had the love of my life too.

After we talked and looked at pictures, he cooked an amazing dinner and we had a delicious dessert. Everything was going great.

"Come in the family room with me Amanda so we can talk."

I followed behind him. I sat on his huge beige sofa and he sat very close to me. He grabbed my hand.

"Amanda, I am so glad you decided to come. This means so much to me."

"I am glad I'm here too Hamilton."

"For a minute there, I thought you would change your mind."

"Why?"

"Just because."

"Because what?"

"Because I am an older guy and you are so young and beautiful."

"Hamilton I am not that much younger than you. So does that bother you because it doesn't bother me?"

"Are you sure Amanda because I feel something for you that I haven't felt in a long time?"

"Hamilton, the question is, are you sure?"

"Baby I mean everything I am saying to you. How do you feel Amanda about me?"

"Hamilton I have not felt like this in my whole life. I think of you all the time and I can't seem to get you off my mind."

"Baby I feel the same way. You make me feel like a new man and I thank God for you."

I don't know why, but tears rolled down my face. I don't know why lately I tend to be so emotional about this relationship. I hope he doesn't think that I am a cry baby or anything like that. Just then he kissed me.

"Amanda, why are you crying?"

"I'm just happy. I didn't think I could ever feel this way."

"You haven't seen anything yet. I am going to treat you like a Queen."

"I can't wait to know how that feels."

"You mean to tell me that you never had anyone treat you special?"

"I have never even seen any man treat a woman like a Queen."

"Really?"

"Yes Hamilton, this is all new to me."

"Baby just let me love you like you deserve to be loved and you will never regret it."

"You said love."

"Yes Amanda, I love you."

"I am so glad you feel that way because I love you too."

We sat there hugging and kissing for what seemed like forever. I don't know, but for some reason I felt really at home with him in his place. He got up and led me into his bedroom. He removed every stitch of my clothing very slowly. We made love for what seemed like hours. Our bodies seem to belong together like pieces in a puzzle. I have never in my life felt so good. He made me feel completely relaxed. I believe that my body has never felt this satisfied in all of the years of love making.

This was so great! I didn't even mind missing our Friday night get together with Colleen and Bobbi. They are the ones who talked me into coming here to be with Hamilton. They said they were still going to hangout though. I can't wait until I get back. I am going to have so much to tell them.

CHAPTER ELEVEN

Roberta

"This is strange being here at Amanda's place and no Amanda."

"I know what you mean Bobbi. But it is still nice to hang out with you."

"I agree Colleen. Even without Amanda we still need a happy hour."

"Exactly!"

"So how is Sabrina doing in school?"

"Girl, I forgot to tell you. She has pulled all her grades up. I looked at her grades on the computer where her school allows parents to check grades and she is doing so much better."

"That is great Colleen!"

"Yes it is. I don't know how she did it, but I just thank God she did."

"I am so happy for her Colleen. I know you were worried about her getting into a good college and all, but it looks like things are turning around for you and Sabrina."

"It looks that way."

"Now all you need is a man."

"Bobbi!" Colleen said and almost spilled the white wine she was drinking.

"Don't "Bobbi" me! Colleen it has been too long for you not to have had a man."

"Did you forget Bobbi that I am a widower?"

"No, I didn't forget. Did you forget that you're still alive with needs?"

"Bobbi I am not like you."

"What the fuck does that mean?"

"I can't have a man anytime I want one."

"And I can?"

"Hell yes you can! Look at you. You are beautiful, smart, and you have that big ass that men love."

We both started laughing.

"Colleen, I'm just saying. It's time you meet someone and have some fun."

"I don't have time for fun Bobbi."

"Girl you have to make time. Look at our workaholic friend. She is having fun in another state. I know if she can take a break then your ass can."

"You're probably right Bobbi, but the pickings are slim around here. Look around. Most all the men in here are with someone or probably just left someone at home on this Friday evening."

"Yes, I have to agree. These are the same men we see every week."

"They are probably saying the same thing about our tired asses."

We both laughed again. This time I almost fell out of the chair.

"Bobbi you probably shouldn't drink anything else tonight."

"Why?"

"Because crazy girl! You almost fell out your chair." Colleen said trying to sound serious in between giggles.

"I'm okay. I probably just need to go home."

"Yes, that's what we both need. It is past my bedtime."

"Colleen it is only 11:45pm, and you don't have anyone to go home to."

"So what Bobbi, I still need to get some sleep."

We couldn't stop laughing.

"You're probably right. Let's pay this tab and go. Unlike you, I do have dick at home waiting for me to ride."

"Well you should be running home for that ride Bobbi. Why did you keep me out this late if Darnell is at your house waiting on you?"

"First of all, I didn't keep you out Ms. Thang, you kept me here. And secondly, I am not in a hurry to deal with him tonight."

"Hold up, I think we need another glass of wine."

"Remember we both have to drive home and we drank three glasses of wine each."

"You're right Bobbi. But seriously, tell me what's up with you and Darnell?"

"I don't know Colleen. It's like I can't get use to a man being there at my place all the time."

"Isn't that what you wanted Bobbi?"

"I thought it was what I wanted until I got it."

"Then what is the real problem? Is he doing what he said he would?"

"Yes, that's it. He is doing everything he said he would do to make this relationship work."

"Again I ask, what's the problem Bobbi?"

"I don't know Colleen maybe it's just me. Maybe I am one of those women who are never satisfied."

"That's not it Bobbi. I think you are just remembering what he put you through and now you're being careful."

"Maybe you're right. Come on let's go.

We both got up and Colleen left the money for the bill on the table.

Tonight was fun. Even though it was a little different not having Amanda there, Colleen and I still had a good time. I am so glad that we each have so much in common with each other that we still have fun when it's just two of us. I am so blessed to have such good friends who I love to hang out with every chance I get. I truly love these women and I don't know what I would do if they were not in my life.

I met Amanda first, and then I introduced her to Colleen. From the moment we met, the three of us hit it off right away. I never thought that I could find best friends at this age in my life. I've had women in my life in my past that I thought were my best friends, but it always ended up in some mess. They either were jealous or on a whole different page than I was. I always wished that I could meet some sisters that were like me. I mean sisters who were professional and had some of the same goals and dreams that I have. But the good part to this is that God not only blessed me with sister friends that I have so much in common with, but sister friends who I share the same spirit with. Sometimes I can't believe how I can be thinking something and Amanda or Colleen will say exactly what I was thinking. That is just how it is with us. There is never any jealousy or back stabbing with us and we are always very considerate of each other. I can call these two women anytime day or night if I need to talk and they will stop whatever they are doing to listen to what is going on with me. I am like that with them too. We don't keep secrets from each other (except that one) and that is why they know all about my crazy relationship with Darnell.

They also know everything about my "no good" father. I know they don't understand why I won't go see him, but they never say anything to make me feel bad. They both grew up with fathers in the house so they can't understand where I am coming from. Their fathers had their issues too, but at least they were there in the house with them. That is more than I can say for Marshall. I don't even know his telephone number. Now that is how I grew up and only a person who walked in my shoes could understand how I feel.

As true to who he is, I see when I pulled up that Darnell's car is gone. Who gives a fuck? I'm drunk and tired!

CHAPTER TWELVE

Colleen

It's Monday morning and back to work. It was a great weekend, especially Friday night hanging with Bobbi's crazy ass. We really had a good time even if we missed Amanda, who should be home today around 3:00 this afternoon. I can't wait to hear all about her trip with "Mr. Right!" I know she is probably still on cloud nine.

Saturday was interesting too. Sabrina and I did work around the house. And for the first time in a long time, she wanted to know about me and her dad.

She said that she can remember all the pain I used to be in and that she remembers the fights and the bruises on my face. (I always thought I covered them up well with make-up.) She said I didn't.

"Mom, I remember you crying all the time and Dad being mean to you or yelling at you."

I sat there at my breakfast table so very quiet. I didn't know what to say to my daughter. But I could see she wanted to talk about this. She needed to talk.

"I am sorry Sabrina for what we put you through for so many years. You are a child and we should have never put you in that mess."

"Mom, I always worried about you. I always wondered if today would be the day that Dad would kill you."

We grabbed hands and started crying. I never knew my daughter felt like this. I guess I never thought about what it was like for her living with an abusive parent. But I should have thought about it. It was exactly how my brother and I felt most of the time growing up.

"When Dad died, I was angry at him and angry at you."

"Tell me why."

"Because I felt like you should have taken me and left. Sometimes you did leave with me, but we would always come back. I know he would promise things would be different. And they would be for only a short period. I felt like he got away with so much by just not dealing with it, even by dying of a heart attack."

"What do you mean Sabrina?" I asked.

"He didn't have to pay for hurting you or taking us away from the family. He never said he was sorry and he just did whatever he wanted and then died. Never paying for the pain he caused us." She said while crying hysterically.

"Baby I am sorry for all of this. Believe me I wanted to run and get away from him, but I was so afraid. Fear will paralyze you and make you think you are stuck. But believe me when I tell you he paid for what he did to me."

She wiped her eyes with her napkin.

"How did he pay Mom? Did you kill him?" She said and we both started laughing.

Isn't it funny how we can be so sad one minute and so full of laughter the next? It was so good to see my daughter laugh after crying her eyes out. I hate that she had to deal with the same things that my brother and I had to deal with. We used to see the bruises on our mother's face all the time. We even saw our father beat our mother until both of her eyes were closed. He was a sick man and he needed help. But my mother, like I, was afraid and ashamed to seek any help.

I made it to my dressing room around 4:45am. Soon after, my makeup artist Shana knocked at the door. (I knew it was her because she always arrives right after I do.)

"Hello beautiful!" Shana said with a big smile as she walked in.

Shana works for the station and has been doing my makeup every since I started here. She is so good at what she does that she has been told time and time again that she could be working for the stars as a makeup artist. And believe me, she has had some days when she had to work miracles on my face after some of the bruises that I've had. But she has never judged me and mainly minds her own business. She once talked about moving to Los Angeles and starting her own business, but when her husband decided not to leave his law firm she changed her mind. I am just glad that she and her family has decided to stay right here so she can keep making me look good Monday through Friday.

"Good morning Shana!"

"Did you have a good weekend?" She asked while setting up her makeup case on my dressing room table.

"It was great! How was yours?"

"It was the same old thing. My husband had a game and the kids and I went with him."

"That sounds like it was fun."

"It was ok. Did you hang with your girls on Friday?"

"Well just one of them. My other friend Amanda was out of town with her new guy so it was just Bobbi and I. We had a great time though. Thanks for asking.

That's the kind of person Shana is. She is so caring and considerate. I am so glad that she works with me.

"Are you ready Colleen?"

"Yes indeed."

She started moisturizing my face before she applied the foundation.

"Colleen, can I ask you something?"

"Yes."

"Do you ever think about dating?"

"Yes I do Shana. Why do you ask?"

"Because my brother is single and I want to introduce you to him."

She has to be crazy. I do not do the hook-up thing.

"I don't think so Shana."

"Why Colleen, you would really like him. He is tall, dark and handsome."

"You're just saying that because he's your brother."

"Yeah you're right, but he is a very nice man and I think you guys would hit it off."

"I'm not saying Colleen that you have to marry him, but he is a very nice man. And I think you guys would hit it off."

"I'm sorry Shana, but I just can't do the hook-up thing."

"Just talk to him Colleen and see for yourself. He is a very nice man and I think you are a wonderful woman. I have been doing your make-up for a long time and you know I know the truth behind this beautiful face."

(I knew she was talking about all the scars she had to cover up after my late husband would beat my ass. She never asked any questions. She just did her job like it was no big deal.)

"I'm just saying Colleen that behind this beautiful face of yours is a wonderful and kind woman. You have been through a lot Colleen and it is time for you to have some happiness in your life. I want you to be happy and have real love like Levi and I have."

She is married to a wonderful man. He is an Attorney and she has offered his services to me many times in the hope that I would be seeking a divorce.

"Let me just pass your number to him and you be the judge after that."

I paused for a moment. Maybe I might have some fun like Amanda is having.

"Okay Shana you can give him by number."

"Great! You won't regret this Colleen."

"Now tell me what's up with him. I don't want any surprises."

"Well he works as a Youth Counselor and he is going through a divorce. He also shares custody of his two kids."

"He's going through a divorce and has two kids!"

"Wait Colleen, it's not a bad situation at all. There is no baby-mama drama and he is an excellent father."

"How old are his kids?"

"They are thirteen and three."

"Oh hell no Shana, I can't do little kids!"

"Wait before you judge Colleen. You should just talk to him and get to know him first."

"Shana something is telling me that this is not a good idea."

"It is a good idea Colleen. Take a chance sometimes. Live a little. Now shut-up and let me finish your face."

What am I about to get myself into?

CHAPTER THIRTEEN

Roberta

I got a call this morning from my sister Dottie saying that she has decided to go see Marshall at the hospital and she wants me to go too. I can't believe she has decided to go. Dottie is harder than I am and she can't stand Marshall or his wife. I told her that I needed time to think about it and check my schedule. (My schedule is really the least of my worries.) I just don't think we should be running out there to see his black ass. I don't remember him ever showing up when one of us were sick.

"Hello, this is Bobbi."

"I am surprised you're in your office."

"Hello Mama, as a matter-of-fact I was just about to leave. I have to be across town in about forty-five minutes."

"Well baby I'm not going to hold you, but I was just wondering if you were going with your sisters to the hospital to see your father this week?"

(Damn! Both of them bitches are getting soft!)

"I told Dottie this morning that I need to check my schedule and get back with her."

My mother was quiet for a moment.

"What's wrong Mama? Why are you so quiet?"

"No reason Roberta."

"Tell me the truth Mama."

"Well I think you really need to go see your father. He is dying baby and I don't want it to be too late."

"Mama please stop calling him my father because he is nothing like a father should be."

"Roberta you are going to have to forgive him one day."

"No I'm not Mama! He let us down! We were his kids too! We didn't ask to be here!"

"Roberta you have to forgive him because you forgave me."

I was quiet then. Tears started running down my face. I hate when I cry about my "Marshall."

"Roberta, listen to me baby. I didn't call you to make you upset. I just want you to know that there aren't any instructions with this match-making and parenting thing. Sometimes we end up loving and having children with people who are all wrong for us. But the way I see it, we were blessed with three wonderful daughters. So I guess God saw something good in him even if it was just his sperm."

We both started laughing then. My mother always knows how to make me laugh when I cry. I love this woman and she has been a wonderful mother. She deserved so much more than a part time lover. I just wish she knew that and would move on from Marshall.

"Mama I love you and I have to go now."

"I love you too pumpkin. But you need to go out to that hospital and say all the things to him that are on your mind before it's too late."

"Let me think about it. I will call you later when I get off work."

"Bye baby."

"I'll talk to you later Mama."

We both hung up.

I had to run in the restroom to fix my make-up before I left the newspaper. Man, I hate when my mother does that. She can start talking about Marshall and get me all worked up. And I can't believe those sisters of mine. They are actually going out there to see him. I thought we were united on this. I know Dottie feels the same way I do, even though she has spent more time with Marshall than Sherry or me.

My mother says that when Dottie was born, she and Marshall had decided to have a baby together. He was going through some things with his wife and decided that once his baby was born, he was packing up all of his things and leaving. He did leave for a short period of time. He stayed with my mother and Dottie until Dottie was almost one. He was never happy however, he soon went right back to his wife and other children. But my mother still had two more children with his ass. I will never understand her thinking. And maybe it's not for me to understand. I just need time to get my head together.

As I was walking out the building my cell phone started ringing. I reached in my purse to answer it, and I could see that it was Darnell.

"Hello."

"What's up baby?"

"I'm walking to my car."

"Where are you off to?"

"Remember I told you that I had a restaurant to review today."

"Yes I remember now. When will you be home?"

"Later on today, why do you ask?"

He was starting to get on my fucking nerves with all these damn questions.

"I'm asking because I had some running to do, but I should be back shortly."

Oh fuck! Here we go!

"What time will you be back?" I asked

"I don't know, probably around seven or eight. I won't be gone long."

"So should I wait up for you?"

"Roberta, I said I won't be out long. Seven or eight is early. You are always up at that time."

"Yeah you're right Darnell. I will just see you then."

"Alright baby. I love you."

"I love you too Darnell."

We both hung up at the same time.

All while I was driving I kept thinking about Darnell. He is such a liar. I know he won't be back tonight and maybe not even tomorrow. But for some reason I am getting to the point of not giving a fuck. He has been sticking to me lately, so it will be nice to just have some air for a minute.

I made it to the restaurant right on time. The food was okay, but I am writing it up as a place to hang out because it is so beautiful in here. Amanda better watch out. Although it's not a soul food place, they do have a pretty good set up there.

Speaking of Amanda, she's back home and I can't wait to get all the details of her trip. We are going to try and hold out until Friday. That means no juicy stuff until we are all together. I know she has a lot to share with us. She texted both Colleen and myself when her plane landed and said that she has so much to share with us about her trip. I just hate we have to wait until Friday.

I made it home around 3:30pm. I didn't see Darnell's car outside so I guess he really won't be home until later. That's cool, I could use the quiet time anyway. I know I told Mama that I would call her back this evening, but I think that I will hold out for a while. All she is going to do is talk about Marshall. I am not trying to hear her mouth right about now. I decided that going to see Marshall is not for me. So I will give her a few days and then I'll tell her. What can she do? She can't make me go if I don't want to. Nobody can.

<u>CHAPTER FOURTEEN</u>

<u>*Amanda*</u>

Although I was only gone for a few days, man there is so much to do here at the restaurant. It's like I have been gone forever. I guess I was gone before I left. Hamilton has truly knocked me off my feet. I have never known anyone so kind and generous. It's like my every wish is his command. I truly feel like a Queen. This is exactly how I feel when I'm with him. I cried when I left. Not because I think I will never see him again, but because I didn't want to leave. Yes, I missed my kids and my friends, but I just wanted time to stand still for us.

Hamilton said he will be here in a couple of weeks. I started counting down the time as soon as I got home. We talked last night until around 2:00am. That's why I am dragging this morning.

I made it to the restaurant around 8:00am and couldn't believe the mess I left in my office. It looks like I ran the fuck out of here. Well I may as well sit down at my desk and get started.

"Good morning boss! Glad you're back!"

"Joe! Come in I missed you!" I said and stood up so I could hug him.

"Don't lie. You haven't thought about me or this place since you left." He said and we started laughing.

"Believe me I have thought of you and how I owe you everything."

"For what, running the place while you were gone? You know it was my pleasure."

"Yeah that too, but I'm not talking about the restaurant. I am talking about Hamilton."

"So you're feeling my boy?"

"Joe, I have never thought men like him even existed."

"What? I'm a man like him!"

"Really, are you serious? I see how you have these women around here jumping all over you."

"That's not my fault is it?"

"Whatever Joe, I'm serious. Hamilton is a wonderful man and I thank you for introducing me to him."

"Amanda you are a wonderful woman and you deserve a man like Hamilton. And anyway it was him who saw you when you walked out. He couldn't take his eyes off you."

"That is so sweet."

"So I take it that you are going to see him again."

"You better believe it! He should be here in two weeks and I can't wait!

"That's great! I am happy for you Amanda. I really mean it."

"I know you do and thanks again. Well enough of that tell me everything that happened while I was gone."

"Didn't you get my emails?"

"No Joe, I'm sorry. Hamilton wouldn't let me read emails or do any work while I was there. I was going to read and answer emails when I made it to the airport, but I didn't have enough time. And then last night, I was so tired dealing with the kids and all, I just decided I would wait until I got here today. Did anything go wrong?"

"No honey, everything was fine. I gave you the rundown in the email. The only thing was that new waitress. She had to leave early two days in a row. She said something about her daughter being sick."

"Did you find coverage?"

"Yes I did. Mary came in early one day and stayed late the next."

"Remind me to get her a thank you card and put a gift card in it."

"See that's what I'm talking about."

"What?"

"You are so kind and generous Amanda. Not many employers will give you a little something for picking up hours."

"Well, it's just a way to show my appreciation. She didn't have to come in, but I appreciate the fact that she did."

"You're right. Well I have a delivery coming in this morning so let me get back out there."

"Thanks again Joe."

"You are more than welcome boss."

CHAPTER FIFTEEN

Colleen

I can't believe I have a date in the middle of the week. It's just coffee, but it's still a date. Phillip is meeting me at this coffee shop not too far from my house. (I didn't tell him that I live in the neighborhood because right now that's not his business.) And besides, this is our first meeting.

Sabrina seemed excited when I told her that I had a date. She said it was about time. However, her enthusiasm had not trickled over to me. I can't believe how nervous I am. We've talked on the phone a couple of times and he seems like he has his head on straight. But in the beginning, so did that crazy ass husband of mine when I first met him.

I decided to dress in a pair of black slacks and a loose fitting gray and black blouse. I didn't want to look too dressy, but not too homely either.

I told him to meet me around 6:30pm and of course he would recognize me. (I'm on television so I know he already knows what I look like.)

I arrived a little early so I could get there and be seated by the time he arrived. I ordered a cappuccino and sat in the middle of the shop. I didn't want to sit in the corner or near the door.

When he walked in my eyes couldn't believe it! I knew it was him because he smiled and waved at me when he saw me. OMG! He was gorgeous! He was dark chocolate with a shaved head. He also had muscles everywhere and a smile that would make you drop your panties on his command!

"Hello Colleen." He said and held out his hand as soon as he reached the table.

I shook his hand.

"Hello, you must be Phillip. Please have a seat."

"Thank you I will, but first let me get a cup of coffee. Would you like anything?"

"No thanks. I have a cappuccino."

"Is it any good?"

"Yes, it's actually great." I said trying not to blush.

"Maybe I'll try one also. Excuse me I'll be right back." He said and walked over to the counter.

I guess it's true what I heard once. That a woman knows if she is going to sleep with a man the moment she makes his acquaintance. As it looks right now, and if he don't do or say something stupid, by the next couple of weeks, he could be the man to help me get over this dry spell.

He made it back in the middle of my daydream. He sat down and took a sip of his drink.

"You were right! This is good!"

"I told you."

"So Colleen is this your favorite little spot?"

"I wouldn't say favorite but I do think it's nice."

"Yes it is nice. I see a lot of people are here with their laptops. Do you work from here too sometimes?"

"No, most of my work is done in my office or at home."

"That's right. You're the early morning news anchor woman."

"That's one way to put it. But I am so much more than just the "early morning anchor woman.""

"I am so sorry. I didn't mean to offend you."

"I am not offended. We just met. How could you know that I was more than a news woman?" I said and we both started laughing.

"Again, I am sorry. Can we start over?"

"I think that's a good idea."

"Have you always wanted to be a news reporter?"

"No, actually I didn't."

"What? You are a natural."

"So you watch the morning news?"

"I do now." He said and took another sip of his cappuccino. "What did you want to do when you were young?" He asked.

"I wanted to be a fashion designer."

"Really, what happened?"

"I couldn't draw or sketch."

"Yeah that would be a problem."

We both started laughing.

"So Phillip, do you like what you do?"

"Most of the time I do. I think I like working with kids the most."

"Really that's interesting? I don't think I could do that kind of work."

"Sure you could. You would fall in love with some of the kids once you get to know them."

"I don't know. It takes a special kind of person to do what you do."

"Maybe, but you would be surprised at what you can do when you are presented with the opportunity."

"I believe that."

We made more small talk for about another thirty to forty minutes. We talked about family, kids and our parents. I kept wondering how much of my background his sister Shana told him. (She assured me that she hadn't and wouldn't tell him about my abusive husband.)

He also shared with me about why he and his wife divorced. I didn't ask but he just went on and on. He said that she didn't want to be married any more. She told him she wasn't in love with him and that he should find someone who could be what he wanted in a woman. From what I could see so far, he seemed like a real catch and any woman would be glad to have him.

"I know that had to break your heart when she said that." I said.

"No not really. She stopped being a wife to me a long time ago."

"What does that mean? Did she stop cooking and cleaning for you?"

"What do you mean stop? She never did those things in the first place. I would go to work, come home and take care of the kids and then cook dinner."

"Wow! That's a lot to have to deal with."

"I think I just got used to it."

I really felt bad for him. If this was the truth then he should be glad that the heifer left. I don't know what's wrong with some women. They can have a good man and treat him like shit, but as soon as he leaves then they want to talk about what they had and lost. I don't know how that feels because my husband was so far from a good man.

We sat for a bit longer. I drank another cappuccino and didn't realize how late it was getting. It was 8:30pm. Damn! We sat in this coffee shop talking for two hours. I don't know when the last time I had a gentleman talk to me for two hours. Not even in my marriage did that ever happen.

"Look at the time. It's getting late and I must get ready to head home." I said.

"Yes it is pretty late. I didn't even realize the time. I guess that's what happens when you enjoy the company you're with." He said with a slight grin.

"I agree. This was nice."

"Then we must do this again."

"Sure." I said and stood up.

"Can I walk you to your car?"

"Yes you can Phillip. That would be nice."

He walked me to my car and gave me a very big hug. It was nice, but a little much for a first date. We said goodbye and agreed that we would talk later.

I pulled off and headed home. As I drove, I thought about what a nice guy he seemed to be. He appears to be smart, caring and compassionate. But believe me I know there are two sides to every story. He probably did all kinds of bad things to his wife. I have never met a man that would even put up with bullshit like that. Take my brother for example. He is a good man, but I know damn well he wouldn't take any shit off of his wife. If he ever felt mistreated, I know he would be gone.

When I pulled in the garage I think I was still smiling. As I opened the door and walked in my kitchen, Sabrina was right there in the kitchen waiting on me.

"Well?"

"Well what?"

"How was your date Mom? Was he cute, nice, and are you going to see each other again?"

"Sabrina slow down and let me catch my breath."

"Wow, he took your breath away!" She said laughing.

"Don't be funny! I'm just saying I had a good time."

"Are you going to see him again?"

"Maybe if he calls and wants to see me again."

"He'll call again."

"How do you know Ms. Grown ass?"

"Because just look at yourself Mom. You are beautiful, smart, and you have a big ass."

"Whatever Sabrina!" I said and grabbed her tight.

"Seriously Mom, you are a catch. And one day there is going to be a man who is going to appreciate you and treat you like a Queen. Now let me go so I can get ready for bed."

"It's still early. Are you going to have dinner with me?"

"I already ate."

"Well did you save me anything?"

"Yes I did. I cooked Sloppy Joe sandwiches."

"Thank you. I love you Brina."

"I love you too Mom."

We kissed and she ran up the stairs. That is funny and life can be funny. Even my sixteen year old daughter knows that a woman should be treated like a Queen. I wish I knew that when I was her age then maybe I wouldn't married an abusive man. Damn I love that girl!

CHAPTER SIXTEEN

Roberta

I am so glad it is Friday. But as usual, Darnell has been disappearing again and lying all the time. I swear I would dump his black ass if I could find another man that could put it down like him. But in the meantime, I keep wishing and secretly hoping that one day he realizes that he wants to be with me and only me. I'm not saying that I want him forever, but it would be nice to have someone to just be with when I chose to.

Take Amanda for instance. She has something great with Hamilton. It is amazing how she found true love when she wasn't even looking. She calls him her angel. Wow! Am I even worthy of having an angel like that? After all, I have done some bad things in my past. I think of the married man that I was messing around with for all those years. (I try not to think of Ron too often.) Yes, I knew he was married, but I also knew he wasn't happy. When we got together, it just felt right. I wasn't sure why it happened, it just happened. I thought I was in love with him and he made me feel so special. Then when I ended up pregnant, it all hit the fan.

That abortion is something that I still regret. How did I ever make it through that? I still have never told my girls about Ron or the abortion. Some things I think they won't understand. They both are mothers and they loved being pregnant. How do I look them in their faces and say to them that I killed a baby. Maybe they will not look at me the same way after I tell them the truth. I just don't know how I would even start a conversation like that. There has been so many times when I have cried myself to sleep thinking about how my life would have been if I would have kept the baby. I probably would have been a single mom, but I was raised by a single mom and for the most part I turned out ok. Maybe that's why I didn't want to keep the baby. Truth is, I never wanted to have a baby by a married man like she did. So telling them the truth is not an option right now and especially not tonight.

I hope today flies by so I can get drunk with my girls. I do believe we have a lot to catch up on. Colleen said she has something to tell us both tonight and Amanda is feeling us in on her trip. And I can always bitch about Darnell or talk about how my mother still loves a man who has a wife and kids.

I had to drive downtown to the opening of a new gourmet sandwich shop to review. One day I just know that I am going to be as big as a house with all this food I eat. I make it a point to never clean my plate, but sometimes it's hard. Some of the restaurants are really great. The food is good and they are more than welcome to give me plenty to sample.

When I walked into the restaurant it looked more like a coffee shop than anything. Maybe that's the look they were going for. That look seems to be very popular lately. It was clean and very well lit. The hours of operation were from 11:00am to 2:00pm. It was only open for lunch. That I found not so interesting. I know some people who will stop and grab a sandwich after work for dinner sometimes. That is something I do often.

I took a seat by the window. I don't believe that anyone was expecting me because no one came out to greet me. So maybe I should just sit here and wait on a waitress. There was only one waitress in sight and I could see that she was busy with a table in the back. She didn't see me come in because her back was to me. One waitress was not good. What if they get a lunch rush?

I decided to pull out my iPad to write down some notes. Just as I looked up, the waitress was coming my way and I could see the couple she was waiting on before she left. (She was blocking my view at first.)

OMG! It was Darnell and some young white woman! We locked eyes. That fucking bastard! Oh what do I do now? I am pissed, but I don't want to make a scene. Now his ass is headed this way. And so is the waitress.

"Sorry about the wait. Can I take your order?" The waitress asked.

"No, I am sorry. I won't be staying." I said while standing and grabbing my stuff.

"Wait Roberta, let me explain." Darnell said while running after me.

"Darnell get away from me. I can't believe I fell for all of your lies again. Move out of my way." I said and pushed him out of the way while I walked out of the door.

"Roberta, it's not what you think!"

"It never is Darnell." I said still walking to my car. I know if anyone was looking they would assume I was running away from a man who was trying to assault me. Then I stopped and turned around and looked him dead in his face.

"You know what Darnell? I'm not even mad at you. This is my fault. I should have never allowed myself to fall for you again."

"Roberta, let me explain. That girl means nothing to me. It's a business lunch."

"You must think I'm stupid. Or maybe I have been just playing the stupid role so long that I do appear stupid."

"I don't think you're stupid Roberta. Please don't leave yet! Let me just talk to you."

"The only thing we can talk about is when you can come and get your shit out of my house."

"Roberta please."

"That's funny. You really think that my name is Roberta Please." I said and grabbed my car door. "Now move your ass Darnell before I get in this car and run your cheating, lying, broke ass over."

He looked in my face and jumped out of the way. He knew I wasn't playing.

I drove off and burnt rubber out of there. Fuck! I hate feeling played! I should have known that he was with another woman. I guess I just ignored the signs. Now I have to go home and gather up another man's belongings out of my house. When will I learn? Just then my eyes filled up with tears. Here I go again crying over a man that can't or won't treat me the way I deserve to be treated. I swear I need someone to knock me in my head right about now. Now I was crying hysterically and I couldn't hold back. But thank God I was only a block from the hair salon. I have an appointment today for 2:00pm, but I am sure Tammy will get me in early if she's not too busy.

When I walked in the salon, I still had my shades on and I headed straight to the rest room. Tammy waved at me as I headed in that direction.

When I walked in the rest room, it was empty and that was cool. I stood in front of the mirror and removed my shades and cried even more. But why was I crying when I expected this anyway? I knew it was only a matter of time before I figured Darnell out. But why does this keep happening to me? When will I find my true love and is there such a thing as true love?

Just as I was asking myself that question Tammy walked in the bathroom.

"Bobbi, are you alright?" She asked and grabbed my hand.

I looked at her and fell in her arms crying as if my whole world just ended.

"Oh no, Bobbi what happened? Is something wrong with your mom or sisters?"

I pulled away and grabbed a paper towel.

"I just caught my man with another woman."

"Really, where was he at?"

"At this nice little cozy sandwich shop a few blocks from here."

"I am so sorry Bobbi to hear that."

"Thanks Tammy, but I'll be okay. Just give me a minute to pull myself together and fix my face. Can you squeeze me in early?"

"Of course honey, anything for you."

"Okay thanks Tammy. You are wonderful."

"So are you Bobbi, but you just don't realize it yet." She said while hugging me again.

"I'll wait on you at my station. There's no rush so take your time."

Tammy walked out of the restroom, but I stood there looking at myself in the mirror for a few moments longer. At this moment, at this present time, I can understand exactly why people commit suicide. At this moment I feel so alone. Even though I know I have people around me who love me, but right now alone is how I feel.

I washed my face and reapplied my makeup and headed back out to Tammy.

"You okay sweetie?" She asked.

"Yes Tammy I am fine."

"Good. I am going to make you look so beautiful that you won't even have time to think about a man."

"How will you do that?"

"When we concentrate on our own qualities and the beauty in us, we take the attention off of all the things that bring us down."

"Now where did you learn that?"

"I learned it at a session of the "Queen's Project.""

"Oh yeah, that is the support group that you attend." I said in a sarcastic manner, although I really don't know why I was being shitty with her when she was being so nice to me.

"I'm sorry Tammy. I didn't mean that."

"I know Bobbi. And for the thousand time it's not a support group. Now come on and follow me to the sink so I can wash your hair."

I followed her to a sink that was right across from her station. She put that apron on me and began to wash my hair. As she was washing my hair I closed my eyes. It felt like she was massaging my head. It felt like all of my problems were being washed away. (I wonder if she learned this too in her group.) The shampoo tingled and smelt like mint as she lathered up my hair. I could have really relaxed and went off into a deep sleep if it wasn't for Tammy running her mouth so much about this "Queen's Project."

"You should really come one day Bobbi and just check it out for yourself."

"Maybe I will. I'll get the address from you before I leave."

"I think I have a flyer here with the information about the program and the facilitator's info on it."

"Cool."

I wasn't sure why I said I would go, but you never know. I need a change and it seems to be doing wonders for Tammy.

Tammy used to live in a shelter and spend most of her young life in foster homes. She says she has done everything to survive and then some. I truly admire her determination and drive. She finished high school and went straight to cosmetology school and graduated at the top of her class. She started doing hair right after that and it has been a very successful business for her. She owns her own home and travels every year to some exotic place.

She finished my hair and I loved it of course. She always does a great job on my hair. I really liked what I looked like in the mirror when she got finished. This young girl really knows her stuff. She also talked about her mother and the new boyfriend that she has. He is almost fifteen years younger than her, but she said if her mother is happy then she is happy for her. She made me smile so much that I almost forgot about Darnell.

Almost!

CHAPTER SEVENTEEN

Amanda

"Baby I really have to hang up this phone now. The girls will be here soon and I need to finish up some work before they get here."

"I know Sweetie, but I just hate to hang up."

"Hamilton you are so funny. We have been talking for the past hour and a half. One would think that neither of us have jobs at all."

"That's true Amanda we do have work to do. I need to make my plane reservations as soon as we hang up."

"Yes you do and I can't wait to see you."

"Are you sure you are ready for me to meet your kids?"

"I already told you Hamilton that they are ready to meet mommy's boyfriend."

"But did you tell them that I'm staying there at the house?"

"Hamilton, don't worry. They are only going to be home the first night anyway and then they are off with their father. Stop worrying."

"I just don't want anyone to be uncomfortable."

"You let me worry about that and you just hurry and get here."

"Woman I tell you."

"What?"

"You got me felling like I am a teenager here."

"Is that such a bad thing? I feel the same way."

"Let's hang up now Amanda. You have a good time with your friends tonight."

"I will and you have a good time playing poker with your friends tonight too."

"I'll talk to you later sweetie."

"Good-bye Hamilton."

We hung up. This man has me on cloud nine! I don't know how the fuck I can get anything done when I am always thinking of him. He says he thinks of me throughout the day too and now he is coming back to visit me soon. This time he is going to meet my kids. This is huge! He will be the first man that I have brought around my kids. (I hope the last one.)

I need to finish up my work and then get out there and wait on my girls to get here. I know that there is a crowd starting to form so I better get our seats by the stage. I am so thankful that Joe is here managing things even when I'm in the office. He manages the cooks, the waitress, and the bus boys. I never worry as long as Joe is on the job.

As I walked out, I looked around and saw that it was packed just like I thought. This doesn't happen often this early on Fridays but I appreciate every time my place is full. That shows me that I must be doing something right. My parents would be so proud

And in the middle of all of these wonderful customers, I see my two best friends sitting at our table sipping on Cosmos. I am so blessed! I have the two most wonderful friends in the world. This is what life is all about. Having love in your life and giving love back. I walked up to the table where they sat.

"Girl, what took you so long to bring your ass out here?" Bobbi said and stood up to hug me. Colleen followed suite.

"It's good to see you too Bobbi."

"Sit your ass down and tell us what you were in that office doing this late on a Friday night, our Friday night?" Colleen asked.

"Ladies calm down! I was just finishing up some work that I didn't get done earlier."

"Too busy talking to Mr. Love Man."

"No Bobbi, for your information smart ass. I talked to him earlier."

"Of course you did."

"Shut-up Colleen, did you guys order anything to munch on yet?"

"No, we were waiting on you." Bobbi said.

"Okay let me go put our order in and I'll be right back. I'll get the usual. Potato skins, popcorn shrimp, catfish nuggets and spinach dip, and of course more cosmos. So sit here and chill and listen to my great band until I return." I said and walked back into the kitchen.

"So Colleen, what is this news that you can't wait to tell us."

"Bobbi, just wait until Amanda comes back and then I will tell you both at the same time."

"Damn Colleen you act like you hit the fucking lottery of something!"

"Maybe I did Bobbi."

"Are you seriously going to make me wait?"

"Yes Bobbi I am. But here comes Colleen now so now I will tell you both."

"This better be good Colleen."

"It is good. Just trust me."

"Okay, I put the orders in now let's get this night started." I said as I walked back to the table. "But first I want to make a toast to my two best friends. I love you both and I don't know what I would ever do without you guys."

We all tapped glasses.

"We love you too Amanda." Colleen said.

"Yes, same here. And now Colleen has some news to share with us Amanda."

"Of course she has news."

"Ha-ha, very funny ladies! Well I want you two to be the first to know that I met someone and I have been on a couple of dates with him.

"OMG! That is so wonderful! Tell us all about him!" Bobbi screamed.

"Well my make-up artist introduced us. We met for coffee and have been talking ever since."

"Is he cute, tall, black or what?"

"Yes Amanda he is all of those things. But most of all he is a very kind gentleman."

"That is so sweet!" Bobbi added. "When do we get to meet him?"

"I don't know yet. I am still feeling him out. But as soon as I see where this is going then we will see."

"Whatever Colleen, just tell the truth. You are waiting until you fuck him to see if you are going to keep him around or not!"

"Amanda that's not true!"

"Yes it is Colleen! You just want to know if he is any good in bed and then you will make your decision."

"Now Bobbi you are wrong too. Both of you guys are wrong for saying that."

"But you know we hit the nail on the head."

Bobbi and I gave each other a high-five and we all started laughing.

"Forget both of you bitches! I am not like that."

"Colleen, no one said anything bad about you. We just know your ass."

"Forget you Bobbi and you too Amanda. I guess you two know me after all." We all started laughing really hard.

Even though we teased Colleen, Bobbi and I both know the type of woman Colleen is. She has had secret sexual relationships since her husband died, but just like I said if the sex is terrible she never talks to them again. Maybe that's her way of not getting hurt or too involved. Whatever works for her is fine with me.

We ended the night talking about my trip to Atlanta and what a wonderful time I had. I also told them that Hamilton and I both confessed our love for each other and they both were really happy for me. However, I could tell that something was going on with Bobbi, but she didn't say anything. She just seemed a little distant most of the night. Maybe she was thinking about her father and the fact that he is sick. I didn't say anything though. I figured she would tell us when she was ready.

We laughed for the rest of the night and also had a few more drinks. The night ended around one o'clock in the morning. This was a great Friday!

CHAPTER EIGHTEEN

Colleen

I can tell that this is going to be a great week already. Phillip has been so nice ever since we met. This Thursday I am going over to his house for dinner. It will be just us, (no kids) but I still don't think I am giving him any just yet. Maybe I will very soon, but not this week.

Sabrina is spending the night at my brother's house on Thursday because she doesn't have school on Friday this week. So I could easily have him over to my place, but I am not ready for him to know where I live. However this works fine, I can leave his house late and not have to worry about getting home to Sabrina. I won't stay long, but I can still chill and relax.

I made it through the week and to Thursday without any major problems at work or at home. Sabrina left as soon as she got out of school so I told Phillip I would be there around 6:30pm. He was cooking spaghetti and meatballs. His kids are with their mother so we will be all alone.

When I got to his house I was kind of disappointed. He told me that his house was small, but that was an understatement. I think you could pick up his whole house and place it in mine.

I got out and walked up to his door. He opened it before I could knock.

"Hello Beautiful."

"Hello Phillip, how are you?"

"Good! Come on in."

I walked through his front door.

"I hope you didn't have any trouble finding my place." He said.

"No I didn't have any trouble at all. I used my GPS in my car to find it."

"Have a seat. Can I get you something to drink?"

"No I am okay." I said while looking around at his place. He walked in the kitchen as if to get me something to drink anyway. I sat down on his couch which looked like it had to be at least twenty years old. He had a couch and a couple of chairs and a big screen television in his living room. He must really be struggling with this divorce and everything because all of his stuff looked really old.

"I know you said you didn't want anything to drink, but I bought you a bottle of water anyway." He said and handed me the water and turned and headed back into his kitchen. I stayed in the living room where I was sitting.

"Thank you Phillip."

"I hope you like what I cooked. I used an old family recipe that is always a big hit." He yelled from the kitchen.

"Phillip you didn't have to go to any trouble for me."

"It was no trouble at all. We both have to eat right?" He said as he walked out carrying a basket of bread.

"I guess you're right." I said.

"So make yourself at home while I set the table so we can then get ready to eat."

He walked back into the kitchen and I started to look around his house with my eyes. I couldn't find anything in here that would be considered quality of even close to it. All of his things looked second hand. Don't get me wrong, there was a time when I didn't have much either. When I was in college and living on my own, I had a sofa bed and a hot plate in my living room. But again, I was in college. He is damn near forty.

"Dinner is served." He said as he put the food on the table.

I walked in his direction. "Wow, everything looks so good Phillip."

"I hope it taste as good as it looks."

"What, you don't you trust your own cooking? If not maybe I should think twice about dinner." I said and started laughing.

"Very funny Colleen, but you know how sometimes everyone else thinks your food is the bomb and you think it's just okay?"

"Yes, I know that feeling. Some things I cook are just meals I threw together, but other people will taste my meals and swear I took my time with them."

"So you're saying you're not a good cook?"

"No I'm not saying that at all, I'm just saying I do okay."

"I bet you can throw down."

"Like I said, I do okay. But if you really want some good down home soul food, you really have to go to my best friend Amanda's spot. Now she can throw down and so can her top Chef."

"Oh yeah, that's right. You said that your girl owns that soul food restaurant."

"Yes she does and the food is delicious. You should stop by sometime."

"I would love to, but I know Fridays are girl's night out. So any day but that one would be okay." He said and started laughing.

How beautiful this man is. He has a smile with pearly white teeth. I still don't know how any woman would leave him. But again, there are two sides to every story.

We made small talk as we finished dinner and to my surprise the food was wonderful. He was a very good cook. He even had the right type of wine with what he prepared for dinner. I was impressed.

I couldn't believe how wonderful everything was with Phillip. He didn't have much, but he sure knew how to make a woman feel good.

I hadn't planned on sleeping with Phillip. But after we ate dinner and listened to a little Barry White I guess you can just say one thing lead to another and we ended up making love right there on his couch in his living room. That same couch that I said looked twenty years old, but now I didn't mind at all. He made love to me like he was a master at it. Our bodies connected to each other like magnets. Never have

I ever felt like this before. I don't know what was happening to me. And when we finished, he held me and kissed me like I had never been kissed before either. I went home feeling better than I had in years. I walked in my house and took a nice hot bath. Wow, was all I could say over and over again. I couldn't wait to tell my girls all about my night, but it would have to wait until Friday.

By the time I made it to work the next morning I was still on cloud nine. Not only had Phillip put it on me, I ended up talking to him until we fell asleep on the phone. It was like we were kids. It had been almost twenty years since a man made me feel this special. I remembered it was back when I was around fifteen and I met the boy of my dreams.

I was at the mall with my girlfriends and the finest boy walked by. He smiled at me and I smiled back. My friends dared me to follow him and get his name and number. I did and we ended up talking everyday on the phone. Sometimes I'd even sneak out the house at night to meet him at the park by our house. Our relationship was sweet and innocent. He was the first person I ever had sex with and he always treated me with kindness. His family moved away my junior year of high school and we never saw each other again. Of course we wrote letters and there were phone calls in the beginning, but soon we both moved on. I went to college and he became a Marine.

It's strange how some situations in life make you remember the sweetest times in your life when love was young and innocent. That is the feeling that Phillip is giving me right now. I thought I would never feel this way again. After marrying an abusive man I never in a million years thought I could be happy or even close to feeling happy.

But as I sit in my make-up chair at 4:30am that is exactly how I feel. I feel happy. Finally this could be the life I always dreamt of having. This could be the man that God Himself picked for me.

"So I take it that smile on your face has something to do with my brother." Shana said as she walked in.

"You could be right."

"I am right! He is always smiling too lately."

"I hope so Shana, because I haven't been this happy in a long time."

"I'm glad Colleen. You deserve to be happy. You both deserve to be happy."

Shana was right. We both deserve happiness.

"So my brother tells me that you guys are getting very close." Shana said and sat in a chair next to me.

"I guess you could say that. But right now we are taking things slow."

"So you guys haven't met each other's children yet?"

"No not yet. But I told Sabrina all about him."

"And how does she feel about you seeing someone?"

"She is so happy for me. She says she likes to see me smile."

"Colleen I am so happy for you. I know how important it is for your daughter to approve."

"It is Shana. She has been through so much and I am not going to do anything to make her unhappy again."

"That's good Colleen and seeing you happy is all the remedy she could ever need."

"I hope you're right Shana."

"I am right. That's the same thing I told my brother about his situation. Once his kids see that he is happy then everything else will fall into place."

"I trust that Shana. But in the meantime get busy and make my face look like I had at least eight hours of sleep last night."

"Will do."

CHAPTER NINETEEN

Roberta

How do I tell the girls that I am not going to make it this evening? This will be the first time I have had to cancel a Friday night. I decided to check out the group that Tammy is always talking about. She called me twice already today literally begging me to come tonight. So what the hell, I can go for an hour or so then leave if it gets too boring. But first I need to call the girls and let them know that I am not going to make it tonight. Last week was so nice that I didn't even get a chance to tell them about what Darnell had done. It was just so nice to hear about Amanda's trip and also to hear that Colleen met a new guy. I felt that the timing was not right for me to put a downer on the night talking about how my heart was breaking and theirs' was just opening up. I will tell them another time.

"Hey Amanda, what's up?"

"Nothing much Bobbi, I just got off the phone with Hamilton. You know I just can't get enough of that man. He will be here soon and I can't wait to see him. I miss him so much."

"Amanda that is so sweet. I am so happy for you. You are a good person and you deserve a good man."

"Thank you Bobbi. So what time do you think you will make it here tonight?"

"Well that's why I'm calling Amanda. I'm not going to make it tonight."

"Why? Is everything okay?"

"Yes, everything is fine."

"Then why are you canceling? You have never missed a Friday. Now tell me the truth."

"Nothing is wrong Amanda. I am just going to go with my beautician Tammy to this group tonight."

"Oh that women's group you told me about awhile ago? The Queen's Project or something like that."

"Yes, that's exactly right. It is called The Queen's Project and each week they discuss different topics that can help empower women."

"Well it does sound interesting, but I want you to be here with me and Colleen. Friday won't be the same without you."

"Don't be so fucking dramatic Amanda. It's just for this week. Next week we will be back to our usual routine. Drinking and talking shit!"

"Did you tell Colleen?"

"No not yet. But I am going to call her as soon as we hang up."

"Okay. Well have fun and try and learn something that you can come back and share with us. Hey, before we hang up, what happened with Darnell?"

"Girl, I caught his black ass with another woman."

"No! Bobbi I am so sorry!"

"I am too."

"But you know that's strike three. You need to kick him to the curb."

"I know you're right. But in the meantime, in between time, I'm going to be all alone."

"Seriously Bobbi, you have been alone anyway. He keeps letting you down and you have too much going on for you to have to deal with his foolishness."

"It's hard though Amanda. I keep wondering why I have never been enough for him."

"That's not a reflection on you Bobbi. There has to be something wrong with him and it's the same thing that was wrong with my ex-husband. They just need more than one woman."

"It sure seems that way."

"So is that why you're going to this group tonight? To help you feel better about yourself?"

"Maybe, I don't know for sure. One thing's for sure though, I am looking for a way to not feel so bad anymore."

"Well Bobbi if it is any consultation, I think that you were always too good for Darnell.

"Amanda no one's better than anyone else."

"No Bobbi, that's not what I'm saying. What I mean is that out of the three of us, you are the one with the most style, the most class, and you are drop dead gorgeous."

"Amanda you are so crazy."

"No Bobbi, I am serious. Now hang up and call Colleen and let her know that you aren't coming tonight. Also, don't forget to call us tomorrow and tell us about your night."

"Thanks Amanda."

"You don't have to thank me Bobbi. You are my girl and I love you."

"I love and appreciate you too."

"Bye."

"Goodbye Amanda."

"Hey Colleen, what are you doing?"

"Nothing much, just cleaning up this kitchen that Sabrina left a mess."

"Where is Sabrina tonight?"

"She is at my brother's house again. It seems she is spending every weekend over there lately."

"You don't mind?"

"No I don't. It has actually been good for her and she seems like she lives for the weekend so she can hang out with my niece Novi."

"That's nice Colleen and I am glad to see that she is doing a lot better these days."

"So what's up with you Bobbi?"

"I am not going to make it tonight for our Friday girl's night."

"Why? Is everything okay with your father?"

"I guess. Why did you ask that?"

"Because you told us he was not doing well so I assumed he was the reason you were canceling on us."

"No, he's not the reason. And anyway I wouldn't miss our night for him."

"Bobbi no matter what, he's still your father."

"That's only because he donated his sperm to my mother's vagina."

"Girl you are so crazy. You always make me laugh. Well if Marshall's not the reason then what's up?"

"I am going to that group I have been telling you guys about."

"That is the one that Tammy told you about?"

"Yes, it's called The Queen's Project."

"So you decided to go today?"

"No I have been thinking about it for a while now, but after the week I've had, I could really use a self esteem boost."

"You can get that from us at the restaurant."

"I know, but I told Tammy I was coming so I am going to just go check it out."

"Well you tell Tammy that she is just borrowing you tonight because Fridays belong to us."

"I will let her know. Oh yeah before I hang up, what happened on your date with Phillip?"

"Well I was going to share with you guys tonight about my hot night."

"Hot night, did you sleep with him?"

"Of course I did."

"You are such a whore! I am so happy you can now put that vibrator up for good."

"You're crazy Bobbi! But you are right. This man rocked my world. Not just sexually, but also mentally. I can't get enough of him. I mean we talk on the phone all the time. If we're not talking then we're texting each other."

"Sounds like you're really digging him. Are you sure this has nothing to do with the fact that you have been alone for a while?"

"No Bobbi that's not it. I really like him."

"Well I think that's cool but be careful."

"I will and everything is great with him so far. But he is a little insecure and wants to know my every move."

"Really, that's kind of strange for him to be insecure so soon don't you think?"

"Maybe he's just thinking about his last relationship and the things that went wrong there. I keep assuring him that not every woman is out to hurt him."

"I hope he knows that. If not, you have your work cut out for you. It's a lot of work trying to get a grown man to believe that you are down for him."

"I don't know Bobbi, I find it kind of cute."

"What's cute about it?"

"Because he really wants me to know that he is in to me."

"I think you just want to know that there is someone who is crazy about you."

"I wouldn't say that, but I do like the fact that I have finally found someone who is crazy about me."

"That's cool."

"Oh yeah, I forgot to ask about you and Darnell. Are you going to talk to him again?"

"No Colleen I'm done. I can't keep doing this back and forth shit with him."

"I understand, but you have said that before. What makes this time any different?"

"I know I've said this before but something inside of me is telling me that this is it."

"Well whatever you decide, I am always in your corner."

"I know that Colleen and I appreciate that."

"I know you have to go, but before we hang up can I ask you a question?"

"Yes."

"Are you going to go see your father?"

"I hadn't planned on it. Why do you keep asking me about him?"

"Because Bobbi, I think you need to go see him so you can get closure. You need to say all the things to him that you always wanted to say."

"I don't have anything to say to him."

"Yes you do Bobbi. Tell him all the things you have always wanted to say. He's in the hospital so he will be right there listening. He can't get up and leave so tell him all the things you say to Amanda and me when you get drunk."

"I don't get drunk Colleen and talk about him."

"Yes you do Bobbi. You always mention how he let you and your sisters down."

"Well he did, but there is nothing I can do about it now."

"True, but you can always tell him how that has affected you and your life and the choices you have made."

"Is that something you wanted to say to your dad before he died?"

"Of course, but remember my dad use to beat the hell out of my mother and my brother and me."

"I know that had to be hard."

"It was. I do believe he was the reason why I ended up with such an abusive husband."

"That's too bad Colleen, and I hate to rush you, but I really have to get ready. But as always, thanks Colleen and I will call you tomorrow."

"Okay have fun."

"Bye."

CHAPTER TWENTY

Roberta

I was pretty excited about going to the group tonight. It was probably because Tammy has been so excited about it ever since her first time going. So I guess her excitement has really rubbed off on me.

I arrived at the center where the meetings are held around twenty minutes before the meeting was to start. It was so many cars there that I had to park at the end of the parking lot. I didn't mind though. Even after working out like crazy today at the gym, I could still use more exercise.

As soon as I walked in I saw Tammy sitting at a table in the middle of the room. She started waving me her way as soon as she saw me walk in. I began to walk in her direction.

"Hey girl, I am so glad you made it. I saved you a seat right here next to me." She said as she stood up and hugged me.

"I told you I was coming."

"I am so glad you are finally here. You won't be sorry."

"I hope you're right."

"Have a seat and it should be starting in about fifteen minutes."

"Cool." I said and sat down. I started looking around the room to see if I knew anyone in the room. No one looked familiar.

Everyone was talking to each other and Tammy and I was also making small talk when the facilitator walked out. All of a sudden, all the women in there stood to their feet and started clapping and yelling. I thought that a celebrity had just walked out.

"Please take your seats ladies." The facilitator said as she stood in the front of the room.

"Thank you so much for coming. I am so happy that the room is full and we have so many women wanting to know how to love and respect themselves. For those of you who are here for the first time, I just want to say welcome and thanks for spending your Friday night with me. And for those who have been with me before, thanks for coming back." She said and everyone clapped.

"First of all I want to say this group isn't about royalty. It is called The Queen's Project. However, it is not about being superior to others or thinking you are better than anyone. It's about loving and respecting you first, and then allowing yourself to be loved the right way." She added.

"You are all probably wondering what I mean when I say the "right way". I mean a person will respect you when you demand respect. So many women start off relationships saying what they will never put up with. But as time goes on, you may find yourself in love and putting up with some of the very things you said you would never deal with. You tell yourself that this is all done in the name of love. You also find yourself loving someone more than you even love yourself. Tell me does any of this sound familiar ladies? Have you ever found yourself so into someone that you don't even recognize yourself or what you are doing? This happens when we don't put our needs first. I am not saying that you should be selfish. I am just saying that if you communicate and be honest with yourself about what you need in a relationship, then you will always come out on top. But I tell you right here and now, this is so hard to do when we are all into someone." She said.

This woman was powerful and I could see why Tammy and so many of these women come to hear her every week. She held my attention from the moment she started talking. She continued to talk and hit on all types of topics that every woman has probably asked themselves about one time or another.

"A person cannot say they love and care for you and then disrespect you. How is that possible?" She added. In truly loving someone, respect goes hand in hand with love. But ladies I say to you, if we don't find out how to love ourselves first, then we will always end up with someone who treats us like we treat ourselves. If you show someone that you don't care about how they treat you, if you keep putting up with mess and telling yourself that things have to get better because I am here putting up with this and forgiving every mistake. Things won't get better until you get better!" The Facilitator said.

The women in here were all on their feet yelling and applauding. I have never seen anything like this before. She went on with her speech as soon as they sat back down.

"Ladies believe me, I know how it is. I have been exactly where a lot of you are right now. Not feeling worthy and not having self respect. I can remember being so into someone to where I thought I couldn't breathe unless I was near him. I loved him so much I put his needs before my own. I made up excuses when he didn't treat me right. I blamed myself when he slept with other women or when we fought and he would call me out my name. I would be mad but I always forgave him and let him come back. It was because I didn't love myself, so how could I possibly expect anyone else to."

"See ladies, the journey starts when you wake-up. When you wake-up and start to see clearly, you will never allow this type of foolishness in your life. You see Ladies when you wake-up, only those people who help you shine will be allowed in your circle. When you wake-up your eyes are no longer closed. You are done with sleeping. You are not walking around letting any, and everybody use you. But the key is to one day say to yourself and anyone else who will listen, "I am done with not loving me first."

"You have to start telling yourself that you are a Queen and you deserve to be treated as such." She said and the whole room yelled with the mention of them being Queens. Hell I yelled! I never thought of myself like this before.

"Ladies, I am going to be honest with you. The journey is a long one for some, but it is a close one for most. A lot of you women in here tonight are already on this journey. Some of you have already said to yourselves that you are tired and that things are about to change for the better. Then there are some of you here who are still so confused that they may never accept the fact that they are Queens. But as I stand here tonight, I tell you that if nobody ever told you that you are a Queen, then I am telling you now."

The rest of the night was exuberating! By the end of the night, most of us were in tears. I do believe that I have never been so mesmerized by any motivational speaker in my life. I enjoyed this more than some of the preachers I listen to. I can't wait to tell Colleen and Amanda about everything that she said. I am going to call them the first thing in the morning and let them know how amazing this group and the speaker were tonight. They are going to have to come hear her for themselves though. Wow what a night!

CHAPTER TWENTY ONE

Amanda

Man this sucks! Both Bobbi and Colleen have canceled tonight. I can't believe this. This is our first Friday that no one is going to show up.

Bobbi is going to that women's group with her beautician Tammy and Colleen called and said that she is going over her boyfriend Phillip's house. I understand having other plans, but I wish they would have let me know earlier. Hell I could have made other plans too. I would have kept the kids home instead of sending them with their father.

"Hey Amanda." Joe said as soon as he walked in my office.

"What's up Joe?"

"I was just wondering where you and the girls were. The band is about to start and your table is empty. What's going on?"

"They both made other plans."

"Really, that's new. You guys are always down front at your table on Fridays."

"I know right. But what can I say. I missed a Friday also when I went to visit Hamilton."

"Yeah that's true. So I guess I can understand. Well let's not waste the evening. Let's get out there and get the party started."

"Joe you don't have to waste your Friday night hanging with me."

"What are you talking about? I would love to chill with you for the evening. And besides, I don't have any plans for the night."

"What? "Mister love them and leave them" is free on a Friday night. I can't believe it."

"Maybe that's the problem. Maybe I am tired of being this ladies man. I need to change my life."

"Joe I will believe that when I see it. Although I do realize that a good woman would change all that for you."

"That's what I'm talking about. Hook a brother up with your girl Bobbi."

"Are you serious?"

"Yes Amanda I am. You know I've been checking for her for a while now."

"I know you always mention her or you're always playing with her. But I didn't know you were serious."

"Quit playing Amanda. You know I can't take my eyes off of her every time she comes in here."

"You are serious, aren't you?"

"Yes I am very serious. I would like to take her out sometimes and really get to know her."

"If you are serious Joe, then you don't need me. Just ask her out."

"That's easier said than done."

"Why do you say that?"

"I say it because she may not take me serious Amanda."

"That's just you being insecure."

"I don't know if she would date a man like me."

"Why do you say that? Is it because you are always with a lot of women?"

"Yeah, she has seen me with a lot of women."

"Well if you really want her, then you are going to have to let go of all of the women that come in and out of here looking for you."

"I know you're right. Now come on and let's get this party started."

"I agree." I said and got up and walked out of the office with him to the table that I share with my girls every Friday night.

The night went amazingly well. I had a great time kicking it with Joe. We hung out until around eleven. I left and he agreed to close up the restaurant. As soon as I got home Hamilton called, but we didn't talk long. However he did say that he was happy that I decided to still have a Friday night out even though the girls canceled on me. He is such a wonderful man and so understanding. My ex-husband would have never agreed to me spending a Friday night out drinking with a man. Truth be told, he would never have understood me hanging out period.

It looks like Joe is really serious about going out with Bobbi. He spent most of the night talking about how he has wanted to go out with her ever since he first met her. Wow! I never knew Joe was so passionate about anyone. He always has these women around, but they never seem to be more than just friends or women he is freaking with. He said he is willing to give that all up if he had a chance with Bobbi. So the first thing in the morning I am going to call her and tell her exactly what he said about her tonight.

I decided to take a nice hot shower and call it a night, but as soon as I went into my bathroom my doorbell rang. Who could it be at this time of night? As soon as I went to the door and looked out I was knocked off my feet. It was Hamilton! He was standing on my porch with a bouquet of flowers. This man is amazing and I can't believe how happy I am at this very moment! My kids are going to be so happy too. He talked to them on the phone and told them that he was going to take them to see this movie that they keep talking about. I am glad that my children are also excited about his visit. I am so blessed. He not only loves me and wants to spend time with me, but he is willing to spend time with my children. All I can say is that Hamilton is one in a million and I am never going to let him go.

The rest of the night was spent without any talking. We made love all night while looking in each other's eyes. No words needed to be said.

Wow what a night!

CHAPTER TWENTY TWO

Colleen

I am so glad I decided to hang with Phillip tonight instead of going to the restaurant. I hope I didn't hurt Amanda's feelings. As it was, Bobbi was canceling and now I was. But I really just wanted to be with Phillip. When I told him that I was thinking about canceling my night with my girls he was so happy. I think that he really enjoys being with me as much as I do him. I hope it just stays this way. So instead of heading to the restaurant, I just pulled up in my new man's driveway. Again, he answered the door before I could even knock. As soon as I walked in we started kissing and the next thing I knew we were headed up to his bedroom. We made love like we both needed each other so bad. It felt like we both were longing to be in each other's arms. This time we lasted over two hours.

"I am so happy you decided to come over tonight." Phillip said as he kissed me on the forehead as we lay in bed.

"I am too."

"I just wish you could spend the whole night with me."

"I wish I could too Phillip, but I really need to sleep in my own bed."

"It's not like anyone is there baby. Your daughter is with your brother for the weekend, so what's the problem?"

"There's no problem Phillip."

"Then why can't you stay with me all night?"

"I already told you Phillip that I need to be home in case Sabrina decides to come home or cut her weekend short."

"I understand that. Then maybe I should start staying the night at your house. That way if Sabina wants to come home she can because you'll be at home."

"Phillip it's too soon for that."

"It's too soon for what Colleen?"

"It's too soon for Sabrina to see a man in my bed."

"She won't see us in the bed dear."

"You know what I mean Phillip."

"I do, I'm just being silly. But it does make me wonder why I haven't met her yet. Are you ashamed of what we are doing?"

"Of course not Phillip, I enjoy being with you."

"Then what's the problem?"

"I already told you Phillip that there is no problem. I just need to be extra careful with Sabrina. Remember I told you that she only recently started talking to me and being nice to me. I just don't want to rock the boat at home. We are in a good place and I would like to keep it that way for now."

"Don't you think that she will be happy knowing that you're happy?"

"Yes Phillip, I totally agree with you. She knows that you're in my life, but I'm not sure she's ready or even old enough to know that we are sleeping together."

He rolled over on his back and looked at the ceiling.

"What's wrong Phillip?"

"Nothing's wrong." He said as he faced the ceiling.

"Tell me what you are thinking."

"I am thinking about us."

"What about us?"

"I'm wondering if this is all we are going to be to each other. Because truthfully baby, I'm looking for more than a bed partner."

Now he is really messing up the mood in here. Everything was going just fine until he started talking about me staying the night. I'm here now. He should be happy.

"Look baby, let's just enjoy this time that we have together." I said.

"Are you saying that you don't think about a long term relationship with me?"

"That's not what I'm saying at all Phillip. Of course I think about us being in a long term relationship and I think about you all the time. But right now I am enjoying where we are right now."

"I am too, but I just want you to know how much I care about you Colleen. Lately you are all I think about. I haven't felt like this in a very long time. You make me feel alive. And I am not just talking about the sex."

"I agree baby. I'm there too. So let's not waste anymore time talking about this." I said as he rolled back toward me.

"What did you have in mind?"

"Let me show you."

Man I really enjoy being with Phillip but sometimes he really can spoil the mood. It seems no matter how much fun we are having he always wants me to spend the night. I keep telling him that staying the whole night is not an option for me right now. I truly wish I could, but I just can't risk Sabrina knowing that I stayed out all night. I don't think I am ready to let Sabrina know that we are this serious. She is aware that we are seeing each other and yes she knows that we spend quality time together, but I just don't think that she needs all the details. I am truly into him and I know he is feeling me too. I just have to take it slow. I just need to talk to my girls. Wow what a night!

CHAPTER TWENTY THREE

Roberta

Last night was one of the most exciting nights of my life. I never thought that I could feel like this after spending the evening with a bunch of women. This group was amazing and the facilitator was so informative. I have never learned so much about myself in such a short time. She had my attention completely. Actually, she held everyone's attention. She was mesmerizing and seriously on point. She broke everything down and I can't wait to go to the next meeting. I am going to try and talk my girls into coming along with me also. I know they would really enjoy it as I did so I am going to call Amanda right now and tell her all about it. It's Saturday morning and I know she is up with the kids.

"Hello."

"Hey Amanda, are you still sleeping. Get up girl it's 9:00am."

"I am in the bed, but I'm not sleeping. Hamilton surprised me last night and flew in. He showed up at my door when I left the restaurant last night."

"That is so sweet! Well girl I won't hold you. I know you have to get back to your man."

"No girl, hold on. Hamilton is knocked out and the kids are still with their father until later. Let me go in the other room."

"Okay I'll hold."

"I'm back. I had to walk into the kitchen so I wouldn't wake him. He sleeps so soft the slightest thing will wake him. So tell me what's up? How was your night at the women's meeting? I'm sorry, I mean the Queen's Project."

"That's why I'm calling. I need to tell you how great it was before I get too busy hanging with my sisters today. We are doing an early dinner tonight."

"That sounds like fun. Will your mother be there?"

"No just the three of us. I think they want to talk about Marshall and how he is doing lately."

"Is he still in the hospital Bobbi?"

"I guess so. I think he's going to be there for a while. They say he only has a few months to live."

"I am so sorry Bobbi. This must be really hard for you guys."

"Well it is what it is. But I didn't call you to talk about Marshall. I want to tell you about how wonderful the group was last night. I loved it so much! I can't wait to go again and I want you guys to come next time."

"Maybe I will. You sound so excited so that means it must really be a great group. I have not heard this kind of excitement in your voice in a very long time."

"I am excited and I learned a lot. But enough of that, tell me about your surprise. Hamilton really got you didn't he?"

"Yes he did. I hung out at the restaurant with Joe. He acted like he was sorry I had to spend the evening without my girls, so we chilled until around 11:00pm. Then I headed home. As soon as I made it home and was about to shower, my doorbell rang and it was Hamilton standing on my porch with a bouquet of flowers."

"You hung out with Joe? What happened to Colleen?"

"She called and canceled right after you did. She said she was going to hang with Phillip for the night."

"Wow! Don't you think they are a little hot and heavy really fast?"

"Bobbi don't start worrying."

"I'm just saying. This is out of her character."

"Why do you say that?"

"I just think that this guy is trying to take up all of Colleen's time. He wants her with him every moment that she has free."

"Well Bobbi he's just into her. You remember how it was when you and Darnell first got together. You guys couldn't get enough of each other."

"Don't remind me. I should have known he was up to no good even back then."

"What do you mean by that Bobbi?"

"I say that because he didn't really know me in the beginning. What was so great about me that made him want me so bad?"

"Well what was it?"

"It was because he needed me around to constantly tell him how great he was."

"That is crazy Bobbi."

"I know right. Can you imagine how exhausting that had to be for me?"

"No I can't. My ex-husband Clyde was just an ass. He didn't need me around because he was always up to something with other women."

"Darnell was an ass too. But back then in the beginning with Darnell, I couldn't see it. I just thought he liked being around me."

"That is an eye opening experience."

"I'm just glad I finally opened my eyes."

"I'm glad too. Oh yeah, I almost forgot. Guess what I learned last night?"

"What?"

"I learned that someone has a huge crush on you and has liked you for a while now."

"Me?"

"Yes you!"

"Who is it Amanda?"

"You will never guess in a million years."

"That's because I am not going to guess Amanda. Who is it?"

"It's Joe?"

"Joe who?"

"How many people do you know with the name Joe Hudson? Remember my restaurant manager and part time bartender."

"Seriously Amanda, you have to be kidding."

"No I am serious Bobbi and you could have a little more enthusiasm in your voice."

"No disrespect Amanda, but he has been hitting on me for years now. In fact, I think he hits on all women that come in there. If he is not trying to talk to all the women, he has some beautiful chick hanging at the bar. He's a playboy Amanda and frankly I am surprised that you would take him so serious."

"I know you are surprised and skeptical but this man poured his heart out to me all night. He said he has been trying so hard to get you to take him serious."

"How can I take him serious Amanda? He is always with a different woman. I just don't want or need that kind of drama in my life right now."

"I understand completely. But can you at least have dinner or drinks with him?"

"No Amanda I don't think so."

"Can you honestly say you are not attracted to Joe?"

"I don't know Amanda maybe a little. When I first met him I thought he was a good looking man, but when I saw how many different women he dates, I knew then that he was a dog."

"Does that make him a dog because he dates a lot of different women?"

"Yes, because he is probably telling all of them the same things."

"He said he's not. He said he is honest with all of them but he really wants you."

"Do you really believe him Amanda?"

"After talking to him last night, I have to say yes. I believe he really wants to get to know you better. Just go out with him Bobbi and see what can happen."

"I know what could happen."

"What?"

"I will go out with him, look into his deep dark eyes all night, and then end up in the bed with him."

We both started laughing. Because we probably both knew it was the truth.

"But seriously Amanda, I'm just not ready to start dating again. Darnell really took me on a world wind. I just need time to pull myself together. I think going to this group is really going to help me get through this."

"I can respect that. I just want you to find happiness like I have."

"I know you do Amanda. You want that for both me and Colleen. But right now I just need to get into myself for a while."

"That sounds like a great plan Bobbi."

"It is a great plan. But we have talked on this phone too long. I am going to let you go take care of that wonderful man that you have in your bed right now."

"He's not still in the bed. I can hear him in the restroom. But I will talk to you later ok."

"Ok Amanda, have fun. Love you."

"Love you too. Bye."

We both hung up at the same time.

It was getting late so I decided to call Colleen and see if we could grab some coffee early. I don't know why, but she has been on my mind a lot lately. Probably because I think that new boyfriend of hers is needy. I hope she sees that and pulls back a bit.

"Hey Girl, what's up?"

"Nothing much, doing some cleaning and waiting on Sabrina to call and let me know if she needs a ride home from my brother's house. What's up with you?"

"Not much, just wondered if you wanted to get some coffee this morning?"

"That would be great! Just let me call Sabrina and let her know that I will pick her up this evening instead."

"Cool, so should we just say in about an hour?"

"Yes just meet me at that little coffee shop on Third Ave."

"Great, you know that is my spot."

"Yes I know. That's why I said it. And besides they have a mint coffee that I have been dying to try."

"Cool I'll see you then."

"Ok."

It is going to be great to talk with Colleen just one on one. I love Amanda, but she is always looking for the sunny side of the street. Colleen needs to really be careful and not put her all into someone so soon. I know she is lonely and she really wants to be loved, but she just needs to be careful. I don't want her to go through what I went through with that fool Darnell.

I made it to the coffee shop in less than an hour. I didn't see Colleen's car anywhere in the lot so she must be running late. I walked in and ordered my new favorite tea and took a seat by the window so I could see her pull up. I never realized how many people come in here on a Saturday morning. I knew it was busy during the week, but I never come here on the weekend so I didn't know how many people stop in here.

I sat there another twenty minutes and Colleen still hadn't shown up. So I decided to call her.

"Hey Girl, where are you?"

"I am almost there. I was tied up at home talking on the phone to Phillip."

"Ok, so I will see you when you get here."

"Yes I should be there in about ten minutes."

"Great see you then."

"Ok."

That girl is head over heels for this man. I really need to talk to her and quick!

When she walked in she looked like she was a little tired. I've never seen Colleen not look her best, even on the weekend. She had on a warm up suite that looked a size too big and her hair was in a loose ponytail. When she walked up to the table I stood up and we hugged.

"Girl I am so sorry I'm late. Phillip called right when I hung up with you. He was talking about me going away with him next weekend."

"Are you going to go?"

"Yes I think so. I just need to make sure Sabrina is okay with it. Hold on girl and let me go order my coffee. I will be right back."

Colleen really looks run down but she sounds really happy. I guess I was just being silly. She is okay.

"Girl you really need to try this coffee. It is the best I have ever tasted." She said as soon as she walked back over to the table.

"I knew you were going to say that. But tell me about this getaway you and Phillip are planning."

"I am not planning it he is. He just thought of it this morning. He is always tripping about me not staying the whole night with him. So I guess this way he will have me the whole night."

"Is that what you want too?"

"Yes I guess so."

"What do you mean you guess so? Either you want to spend the whole weekend with him or you don't."

"I do want to but sometimes he can be so needy."

"What do you mean?"

"I mean I love being with Phillip and I am so grateful that God sent me someone to be with. But lately I have been spending so much time with him that I have been neglecting some of the other areas of my life."

"You are just going to have to tell him that you need some time to take care of you."

"I tried that. But every time I say that he thinks that I am getting tired of him."

"That sounds like he is more than needy. He sounds insecure."

"I guess you could say he is somewhat insecure. After going through what he went through in his last relationship, I do believe I would be a little insecure too or maybe even a little cautious."

"Cautious yes, but not so worried that everyone was out to get me or do me wrong. And besides, what about all the things you have been through in your past relationship? You should be the one who is cautious."

"I told him that and he understands."

"So are you being careful Colleen?"

"Yes Bobbi I am. You sound like my brother. He asked me the same thing."

"Maybe we are just worried about you."

"Don't be worried Bobbi. I am happier now than I have been in a long time. I never thought I could feel this way."

I looked in her eyes and I could tell that she was serious. I couldn't even imagine how she must feel after being abused for so many years. And who am I to rain on her parade. I am so happy that she is happy. Now I can stop worrying so much.

"Well if you are happy then I am happy for you. Just remember to get you some time to yourself. Don't worry, that dick will be there when you get done taking care of you."

"You are so silly Bobbi." Colleen said and we both started laughing.

CHAPTER TWENTY FOUR

Colleen

Coffee with Bobbi was great. I love spending time with my girls. It seems like we have not had time to just hang out in a very long time. Probably because most of my time is spent with Phillip or working on the next story. But after having coffee with Bobbi, it looks like they understand completely. And besides, they both are doing their own things. Amanda is spending time with Hamilton and Bobbi couldn't stop talking about this new group she went to called, "The Queen's Project." She said that she really enjoyed it and the facilitator really knew what she was talking about. I told her that I would love to go with her the next time I am available.

But truthfully I don't know when the next time I will have some free time. This weekend coming up is my getaway weekend with Phillip and the following weekend I am taking Sabrina and my niece Novi on a weekend shopping spree. My brother and his family have been spending so much time with my daughter, I figured that it's time I spend time with the girls also.

My sister-in-law would go along with us, but her father is moving into a nursing home and she will be helping with that. So taking the girls for the weekend will be a good way for me to spend time with them.

All week long all I could do was think about the weekend. My week started off good but by yesterday morning all that changed.

I arrived at the television station yesterday around 4:30am. I sometimes get there a little early in case I need to go over some things with the producer before Shana gets there to do my make-up.

Chris is a very good and fair producer. He's honest and he tells you like it is.

"Hey Colleen I'm glad you're here. Come in and have a seat."

"Thank you." I sat down in a chair right in front of him.

"I wanted to let you know that next week will be my last week producing the morning news here."

"Wow, what's going on Chris?"

"I got offered a position I couldn't refuse. I am the new producer of the FOX evening news."

"Wow Chris that's great! I am really happy for you. When do you start and who is going to produce the early news now?"

"Well I have to start in a couple of weeks and Maria is going to produce the morning news."

"Maria? Oh no! I can't stand her."

"I know honey, but just think positive."

"I'm positive that it's going to be a mess around here. She gets on everyone's nerves."

"Colleen just remember that she works hard and she has had to work even harder than most men in her position."

"I know Chris, but it seems like she hates me."

"That's not true Colleen. She's just a different kind of person. She's not one of those people who talks to everyone or wants to hang out after work. But we shouldn't hold that against her."

"That's the truth. We invited her out a few times and she always says no."

"Well maybe she's always busy."

"I don't know Chris. She never says that she's busy. She just says "no thank-you.""

"Well at least she's polite about it."

"I guess you're right."

"Anyway beautiful, I'll miss you but you have the number. And any time you feel like hanging out feel free to contact me and Antonio."

"How is the love of your life doing?"

"Girl he is getting on my nerves. You know he lost that last case so living with him is an adventure in itself."

"That was a huge case Chris. I know he was upset about losing."

"True he was upset, but now he's making me upset."

"Just like you just told me about Maria, be patient and think positive."

"I will girl no matter what. I'm not leaving him."

"I know you're not because he's a good man. Now I have to get back to my dressing room."

"Okay dear I'll see you on the set."

We hugged and I left his office.

By the time I walked back down to my dressing room Shana was there waiting.

"I'm sorry girl for keeping you waiting, but I was in Chris' office."

"No problem Colleen. Just have a seat and let's get started."

"Okay."

I sat down and Shana started applying my foundation to my face. She usually would ask me if I have applied moisturizer first. Today I did, but she didn't ask. I guess her mind must be elsewhere.

"Shana is there something wrong?" I asked.

"I am so sorry Colleen. My mind was elsewhere."

"Stop apologizing Shana. It's not a big deal. Just tell me what's going on."

"Okay, I didn't know if I should tell you or not."

"Tell me what?"

"Well, I was at my mother's house last weekend and my brother's ex-wife came over."

"Okay what's wrong with that? Your mother is her children's grandmother."

"This I know. It's not her coming over it's what she said."

"What did she say? Or do I really want to know? Did she say they were still sleeping together?"

"No nothing like that."

"Well what's the problem Shana?"

"She said that Phillip used to abuse her."

"What? I don't believe that! Phillip would never hit a woman."

"No Colleen, she didn't say the abuse was physical. She said he did crazy things to her."

"Crazy things like what?"

"She said he was mentally abusive. He used to lock her in the room and put his gun to her head."

"What? That's hard to believe."

"I know right. My mother and I were speechless. We didn't believe her at first. Then she started crying and said that's why she finally left him."

"My goodness Shana that is crazy. Why would he do something like that?"

"I don't know Colleen, but I feel like she is telling the truth. And I was torn as to if I should tell you or not."

"I am so glad you did. I don't know what to do with this information."

"Are you going to ask him about it?"

"I sure am. I just have to make sure I look him in his face."

"Why do you need to do that? To see if he's telling the truth?"

"Yeah that too, but we made a vow to always talk things over face to face."

"That's good Colleen. I am sorry again for missing the moisturizer on your face and coming in here with this terrible news."

"Don't worry Shana, I'm glad you had that on your mind and I appreciate you thinking enough of me to tell me about this. He's your brother so I know that had to be a tough decision to make."

"It's not that Colleen, I just feel like I owe you that. Not because I hooked you guys up, but because you are a woman. And I owe you that respect."

We hugged and she finished applying my makeup.

For the rest of the day I couldn't help but think about what Shana had told me. If it is true, there is no way I could continue to see this man. What kind of man puts a gun to a woman's head because she wants to leave him? But again, what kind of man beats a woman for all of their marriage? Is this a retake of my life? The first thing I thought about was that I needed to get with my girls and tell them about this. But I didn't get a chance to tell them anything because I called Phillip and we talked about everything. That's why I didn't make my night with my girls. I ended up agreeing to go over his house and I am glad I did. We ended up having a wonderful night and he explained everything to me. There is always two sides to every story and I believe his side.

CHAPTER TWENTY FIVE

Roberta

Sometimes I love hanging with my sisters. Then there are times that I don't. But it is still good to kick it with them. The funny part is we tend to always talk about our childhood and the crazy things we did. Dottie got away with everything because she was the oldest, and Sherry never had to do any work because she was the baby. So you know she was the favorite. That left me in the middle. Now you know how the middle child is treated. I sometimes felt like I got no love or attention. I knew I was loved by my mother, but it would have been great to be the favorite sometimes.

I hope we don't talk about our mother too much though because that conversation could last forever. Once we get started on her we never stop. It's all done in love though. We also laugh about things that our mother used to do when we were young. She used to listen to the same song over and over and do this crazy dance when she had a couple of drinks. It was funny then and we would get a kick out of her. But looking back those were great times. It has been a lifetime since we have seen our mother dance.

We decided to meet at a very nice and expensive hotel downtown. It has a beautiful restaurant located in it and everyone is always talking about how great the food is. I've never been there, but I did plan on reviewing it sometime in the near future.

I arrived on time, but my sisters were nowhere in sight. I wasn't surprised. Sherry is always late dealing with the twins and Dottie has to always wait on her. I didn't mind though. It would give me time to chill and have a glass of wine before they made it there.

The hostess showed me to my table and I ordered a glass of Merlot. Man, this place is beautiful! I should get me a room here one day when I want to pamper myself. I am sure Dottie and her husband has stayed here before. That is the kind of thing they like to do. They are always staying in nice places. They have a beautiful home, but they like to switch it up sometimes. I get it! I think changing up the scene for the sake of romance works out. And they can afford it with no problem.

A waitress brought my drink and a basket of bread. I took a few bites of the bread before my sisters showed up. They walked in together dressed like they just stepped out of Vogue magazine. It is so strange how all of our styles are the same. All three of us can't get enough of designer fashions, none of us will carry a purse that cost less than a couple hundred dollars, we won't buy cheap shoes, and we never leave the house unless our bag matches our shoes. Sherry and I have to look for bargains, but Dottie only shops at the most expensive stores. I waved them my way when I saw them enter.

"Hello Beautiful, I am so glad we are doing this. I really needed to get away from the boys. They have been driving me up the freaking wall." Sherry said.

"Sit down Sherry. You are so crazy. You have two wonderful boys."

"If they are so wonderful, then why haven't their Auntie Bobbi picked up their little asses lately?" Sherry said and we all started laughing.

"Hello Dottie."

"Hey Bobbi, you look like a million bucks as always."

"And so do you both. I am so glad we are here at this beautiful spot. Wow Dottie, this place is the bomb! You chose a great spot. I'm impressed."

"I didn't pick this spot Sherry did. What are you drinking?"

"I'm drinking Merlot."

"That's what I'll have. Where's the waitress?"

"Sherry, tell us how did you know about this hotel?"

"I attended a conference here a couple of weeks ago."

"What kind of conference?"

"It was just some mental health stuff."

"May I take your order?" The waitress said when she returned to the table.

"Oh we're not ready to order dinner yet, but we each would like to order a glass of Merlot." Dottie said.

"Right away." She said and walked away.

"Why would she ask us if we were ready to order before she took our drink orders?"

"I think she meant drinks Sherry."

"Then why didn't she just say drinks in the first place Dottie?"

"I agree Sherry." I said.

"Bobbi you always agree with Sherry."

"Yeah only when she's right."

"Which I usually am always right." Sherry said and we all started laughing.

We made small talk about work, kids and I told them about my breakup with Darnell. I also told them about "The Queen's Project" and how much I learned from the group. They both said it sounded interesting and that they would come with me one night. We talked about our mother and how she has been doing. Sherry sees her the most because she lives in her neighborhood. I truly don't know how she does it. I don't think I could ever live that close to our mother and still be in my right mind. She can drive you crazy and make you want to kill her. We all love her but she can be a bit over whelming sometimes.

"So let's stop beating around the bush." I said.

"What are you talking about Bobbi?"

"Stop bullshitting Dottie and tell us why you wanted to meet for dinner."

"I agree with Bobbi. What's up Dottie?"

"Well to be honest with you both, I thought it would be nice to spend some quality time with my sisters. And secondly, I think that we need to listen to mom and go see Marshall."

"Why?"

"Because Bobbi he is our father and he is very ill."

"Seriously Dottie, remember when you were in the hospital with a broken leg?"

"Yes I remember that Bobbi. Why are you bringing that up?"

"You broke your leg in two places and had to have surgery and you were hospitalized for over a week. I remember mama saying that she told Marshall and he was coming to see you, but he never showed up."

"I remember that too Dottie." Sherry chimed in.

"I do remember that Bobbi. But I never expected him to come see me."

"See that's the problem Dottie."

"What are you saying Bobbi?"

"I'm saying that you should have expected him to come see you. You are his daughter. And as a father he should have been there for you and for all of us for that matter."

The three of us were quiet for a few seconds. I guess they were thinking about what I had just said.

"You're right Bobbi to feel the way you do about Marshall. And Sherry you are right also to agree. But when it's all said and done, we can hate him and really dislike the way he treated us. But there is a woman who has been there for the three of us from day one. She has been a mother and a father to us in every way possible. Now she has asked us to do something. Something none of us want to do, or understand how she can even ask this of us. But in her mind, she thinks that this is something that we should want to do. She loves this man and I know she has to be hurting to know that he is leaving this earth soon.

It's different than knowing that he is across town with someone else, but to know that he is dying has to be hard on her. We don't have any idea what she could be going through right now. She will probably never tell us, but I am sure she is going through her own pain right about now. So if she wants us to go see Marshall before he dies, then so be it. He is our father and we have to do this for her and for us. Because I think if we say no, her heart is going to break. And I won't live with the fact that she asked something of me and I said no. We have not always agreed with the things she did, but she has always loved us no matter what. So Bobbi and Sherry, I need you both to do this for her because she is our mother and she is the one person who loves us unconditionally. Let's put all hurt aside and do this for her. With no questions asked." Dottie said as tears rolled down her face.

We sat there for a minute and watched Dottie wipe her tears away. Soon the waitress came back and brought their drinks and took our dinner orders. We spent the rest of the evening talking about old times. I truly love my sisters!

CHAPTER TWENTY SIX

Amanda

"Baby I hate when you have to leave."

"I know honey, but you will be in Atlanta in three weeks."

"Yes I know Hamilton. But sometimes watching you get on that plane is the hardest thing I have ever had to do."

"Come here baby." He said and pulled me close in his arms.

"Do you know how hard it is for me to leave you? You are the center of my world. When we are apart I think of you all day and night. I don't know how I am able to get any work done at all. Sometimes when I'm in my office, I often find myself sitting there looking at the clock and wondering what you are doing at that same moment. Does that sound like a crazy man?"

"Hamilton that is not crazy because I think of you too. I find myself deep in thought thinking about the last thing we said to each other. Or I'm counting the hours until we see each other again."

"Amanda I don't know how I am going to continue to do this. I have never in all my years been in a situation like this. I can say that it does seem a little odd for a man like me to fall so deep so fast. Sometimes I can't believe that this is me at all."

Oh my God! He is about to break up with me. No, this can't be happening after we spent such a wonderful few days together. He even met my kids. Why did I not see this coming? I knew he was too good to be true. Fuck it! I am going to just deal with whatever he says.

"What's wrong Amanda? You look like you saw a ghost."

"Hamilton I can't believe you are saying this!"

"Saying what?"

"That you want to end this. What about the last few days? And my kids Hamilton, they really like you."

"Come here Amanda and sit on the couch with me."

"No Hamilton! Whatever you have to say to me you can say it while I am standing here."

"Okay Amanda, as I was saying before. I don't think I can keep doing this back and forth thing so I had to make a decision."

I stood there with tears running down my face. Here I go again, crying over a man.

"My decision is." He said and got on his knees in front of me.

"Hamilton what are you doing?"

"What do you think I'm doing?" He said and reached in his pocket and pulled out a small box.

"Amanda again I say, you are the center of my world. I don't want to keep doing this. I love you and I am not leaving this town without knowing that you want me as bad as I want you."

"I do Hamilton."

"Then Amanda my love, will you marry me and make me the happiest man on this earth?"

"Yes, yes, yes Hamilton. I will marry you. Now get off your knees."

He stood up and we hugged and kissed passionately for what seemed like forever.

"What happens now Hamilton?"

"Amanda my love we have to pick a date and a place to get married."

"I know we do. But right now we have to make love before you head to the airport."

"I agree." He said and picked me up and carried me into my bedroom.

We made love like wild animals. Hamilton is a great lover even at his age. He does things to my body that I have never felt before. He is a wonderful man in every way. He takes his time and never rushes when we are together. He looks into my eyes and it is as if he knows exactly what I am thinking. God has truly blessed me! And now this man has asked me to share his life with him. This is a great day.

He must be a great guy. My ex-husband even stated that he seemed like a nice guy and that he was happy that I found someone. He met Hamilton and was very pleasant with him. He even came and got the kids last night so we could spend his last night in town together alone.

"Wow! That was amazing! Woman you're simply amazing!" Hamilton said as I lay in his arms.

"Don't make me blush."

"You are amazing and the most amazing thing of all is that you are going to be my wife."

"Yes I am." I said and held up my hand with the huge ten carat ring that he just placed on my finger.

"Baby I have to get to the airport before I miss my flight."

"Yes I know Hamilton. I just hate this part."

"I do too baby."

We showered together and headed to the airport.

I left the airport and headed straight to the restaurant. I couldn't believe what just happened. Did Hamilton just propose to me and did I just say yes? I guess so. This beautiful ring says I am getting married to the most wonderful man in the world. What could I have done in life to deserve such a wonderful man? I never in my wildest dreams could have imagined a man like this. I am truly happy and I can't wait to tell my girls and I know they are going to be so happy for me. When my ex-husband used to cheat on me with other women, I would think that maybe this is just what men do. I thought I would just stick it out until he got tired. We didn't have real love for each other. I didn't have love for myself either at that time.

As as I drove, all I could think about was how wonderful Hamilton is. *"He actually wants to spend the rest of his life with me"* is what I kept repeating over and over again to myself. God is good and He loves me.

I walked in the restaurant smiling from ear to ear. I spoke to a few of the people in the kitchen on my way to my office.

"Hello Ms. Amanda."

"Hello Candy how's it going?"

"It's going good and I am learning a lot here. This is a great place to work and everyone is so nice and willing to show me everything that I need to know. Again thank you so much for this opportunity Ms. Amanda. I don't know what I would do if I had to go back to that strip club."

Candy was a new waitress that I hired after she came in late one night dressed like a girl straight off the corner. I noticed her as soon as she walked in. It was something about her that said she needed my help and right away. I gave her coffee and talked to her about her life and what she wanted for her future. I was amazed at all of the things she had been through at such a young age. Hell that could have been me if I didn't have the parents or the opportunities that I had. She told me that she had a baby last year and her parents put her out. She needed money so she started stripping and doing other things to survive. It broke my heart right then and there. I could see that she hated what she had done and just needed a break to get herself together. All while we were talking something was telling me that I needed to reach out to this young woman. After all, it wasn't a coincidence that she walked into my restaurant at 11:00pm. God sent this woman here.

"Candy you don't have to keep thanking me. You are a blessing to us. I needed a new waitress. You just showed up at the right time."

"I know that's not true Ms. Amanda, but I thank God for you and Joe every day. He is a nice man and he shows me that there are good men out there."

"Yes he is a good guy. Have you seen him today?"

"Yeah he's in the office. I will talk to you later Ms. Amanda. I have to get back to my customers."

"Alright Candy and keep up the good work."

She headed out to the dining area and I walked in the office to see Joe sitting at my desk on the phone. I didn't mind though, nothing could bother me today. I walked in and hung my coat on the door hanger. I didn't say anything until he hung up the phone.

"Look at you smiling from ear to ear." Joe said and stood up.

"Move man and give me my chair. I am not smiling any differently than I always do. Anyway you are smiling too. Who was that you were just talking to?"

"Guess."

"I don't know Joe. Some new little chick, who just happens to be head over heels for you?"

"No that was your girl." He said smiling.

"Really, that was Bobbi?"

"Yes it was."

"I have been at home for a few days and I miss all the news. Tell me how did this happen? And when did ya'll exchange numbers?"

"About three days ago. I was thinking a lot about her and just decided to call her."

"Really, I didn't know you had her number."

"Amanda you know I can get any woman's number I want."

"So what you're telling me is that you got it out of my phone book on my computer."

"Yeah basically that's what I did." He said and we both started laughing.

"So what happened when you called her?"

"Well at first she didn't know who I was, and then she caught my voice. She had just got in from hanging with her sisters and she was a little stressed about the whole evening."

"Yeah I bet. They can stress her a bit sometimes. So what else happened?"

"Nothing really happened. We just talked for a while that night and we have been talking every day since."

"Wow! Joe I am so happy for you. I truly believe you when you say you really care about my friend. Please don't make a liar out of me."

"I do really care about her Amanda and she is everything I could ever want in a woman. I changed my ways and now I am ready to be with only one woman."

"That's good Joe. I guess everyone finds the right way to live eventually."

"I think she could be the one for me Amanda. This woman has it together."

"Joe what makes her any different from all those other women that run through here? I am not trying to be funny, but I do believe that you have claimed a couple of other women as being the one for you."

"I know Amanda, but this time I am serious. I am not going to do anything to blow this. Well enough about me, when were you going to explain that big ass rock on your finger?"

"What rock?"

"Stop playing. Did he pop the question?"

"Yes!" I screamed.

"Congratulations Amanda!" He said while hugging me.

"Thank you Joe. And thank you again for introducing me to Hamilton. He is a wonderful man and I love him with all my heart."

"Don't thank me Amanda. I feel like you two are meant for each other. I love you like a sister and I love him like a brother. I just thought you would be good together."

"We are."

"So have you guys set a date?"

"Oh no, we just got engaged this afternoon. I don't even know if he's moving here or if I'm moving me and the kids there."

"Well you have plenty of time to work out the details. There isn't any need to rush because that man is not going anywhere. He loves you and he showed you that he is here for the long ride. But in the meantime, I have to get back out there because I have a date and I need to leave early if you don't mind."

"No I don't mind. Tell Bobbi I said hello, but don't tell her about the ring."

"I know that's girl talk and you want to share that with your girls yourself."

"You are right."

"Okay and again congratulations Amanda."

"Thanks Joe and right back at you."

He walked out of the office still smiling. I feel so happy for Joe and Bobbi! Joe is a good guy and that is exactly what Bobbi needs. Finally she would be dating someone who really cares about her. Someone who wants to spend time with her and not be there one day and gone the next.

It is so strange the connection that Colleen, Bobbi and I share. Not many women at our age get a chance to have best friends who they can share everything with. I never thought I would be able to tell anyone about the mess of a marriage I had. They are the only women that I have ever told the truth to. Bobbi said she never told anyone about all of Darnell's lies and I know Colleen never shared with anyone about the abuse that she endured with her late husband. But look at us all now. I am happy and I hope Bobbi will soon be happy with Joe because he is a great guy. And I believe that he would be good for her. And of course Colleen is falling madly in love with her man Phillip. She seems to like him a lot and I am just happy that she is happy. I can't wait to tell them my news!

CHAPTER TWENTY SEVEN

Colleen

This was a crazy a week. I thought I would never make it through this week after what Shana told me. It made me look at Phillip in a different light. How could I be with a man who does crazy things like that? I am so glad I had the opportunity to speak to Phillip about all of this. He explained everything. He told me of how his ex would lie on him and she would file false police reports stating that he had abused her. He said that she would lie about everything. That was one of the reasons he was glad it was over. She even showed up on his job once and told his Principal that he had locked her in the house all weekend and would not let her leave or use the phone to call for help. After talking to him, his Principal could tell that she was lying. The best thing for him he said was when she packed up her stuff and left one day. I know he hated how things ended, but he said enough was enough. He was tired of being made to look like a crazy man. There are some women that lie on men and make up things to get them arrested or out of their lives. I am not like that however. I never made up anything on my late husband. Hell I didn't have to. He was a mean person and just unhappy with himself and everything around him. I was closest to him so he took everything out on me.

I remember one time when he didn't get this promotion that he so badly wanted. He came right in the house and looked at me as if it was my fault. I tried all that night to make him feel better, but it seemed everything I did only mad it worst. Needless to say, I ended up with a busted lip and a black eye. I am so glad that I don't have to deal with anything like that again.

This evening Phillip and I are going to dinner and then to see this Denzel Washington movie that I have been dying to see. Phillip wants to see it too, even though he won't admit it. After the movie I am going to meet the girls at the restaurant and chill for a while. It seems like it has been forever since we last got together. I have been spending most of my spare time with Phillip and Amanda has been with Hamilton when he's in town. Bobbi is really into her woman's group and enjoying every minute of it. So it seems like none of us really have the time to just hang like we use to. That's why tonight is so special. Not only are we hanging tonight, but both Amanda and I are going on Saturday afternoon to an event that Bobbi told us about. It's the same group that she goes to, but on a larger scale. I am really excited about going and it's wonderful to know that a sister is so positive and uplifting. Bobbi said she is funny as hell too. She has also talked both her sisters into going also. I can't wait until tomorrow. It is going to be a very fun afternoon.

I told Phillip that I would be ready by five o'clock, but it is five thirty and he still hasn't arrived. I hope everything is okay. Maybe I should give him a call and see where he is.

"Hello Phillip where are you?"

"I am sorry baby. I had to drop off the kids at their mother's house. I am pulling in your driveway right now."

"Okay the door is open so come on in."

I am going to stand right here in the foyer so when he walks in he can see this new dress I bought especially for him. It's tight and his favorite color blue.

"I am sorry baby." He said as soon as he walked through the door.

"It's not a problem Phillip."

"What are you wearing?"

"What do you mean Phillip?"

"I mean why do you have on that tight ass dress?"

"This dress is not that tight. I thought you would like it."

"I do like it Colleen, but it's not a dress that a professional woman such as you should wear."

"That's crazy Phillip. Let's go I'm getting hungry."

"I'm not playing Colleen. Take that dress off or I'm not going anywhere with you."

"Seriously, you want me to change clothes just to go to dinner and a movie?"

"Yes that dress is inappropriate. It looks like something a whore would wear."

"No it doesn't. I like it and I am not changing."

"Then I'm leaving."

"Fine!"

"Bye." He said and turned around and walked right out of the door.

What just happened? Did this man just walk his ass out of here? I can't believe how childish he was just acting. I think I look hot but classy. What is wrong with his ass? I've never met a man who has such mood swings like he does. I need to call my girls. I will start with Bobbi.

"Hello."

"Bobbi what are you doing?"

"Getting dressed, what's up? You sound funny."

"I can't believe this!"

"Believe what Colleen?"

"Phillip's ass!"

"What did he do Colleen?"

"We were supposed to go out tonight before I hook up with you guys, and just because he didn't like what I had on he got mad and left."

"He what?"

"He left! He just stormed out of here because my dress was too tight he said."

"What kind of dress do you have on Colleen?"

"Stop playing Bobbi. It's tight but it's classy."

"Well maybe he wanted you to chase him."

"Hell no! What would I look like chasing him and saying ok I'll agree with you?"

"It seems like this is some type of control game."

"What do you mean Bobbi?"

"I mean he wants you to look a certain way and dress how he thinks you should dress."

"He just has these crazy mood swings that get on my nerves."

"What do you mean?"

"I mean one minute he's happy and life is good. Then out of nowhere, he's acting as if the world is on his shoulders."

"Really, what's that about?"

"I don't know. He's starting to work my nerves."

"Starting?"

"Yes starting. If he didn't make such good love to me, I would leave his black ass right now. I swear I would."

"Colleen you can't build a relationship on good dick. Besides it seems like he just left you anyway."

"Very funny Bobbi. Where are you about to go? I know we all agreed that tonight is just drinks so where are you having dinner tonight?"

"I have a date."

"With who?"

"I will tell you tonight when I see you both."

"That sucks."

"Why?"

"It sucks because I don't want to wait for hours to hear the news about this new guy in your life."

"Call Phillip back and tell him you'll change clothes."

"Like hell I will! I let a man control me once and I'll be damned if I do it again."

"Then if you feel that strongly you should call him and tell him exactly how his behavior tonight made you feel."

"Do you think he will understand?"

"Do you care if he understands or do you just need him to hear you out? He doesn't have to agree he just has to hear you say it."

"Wow! That group is really changing you."

"Why do you say that Colleen?"

"I say it because you talk with a lot of insight about relationships now."

"I don't think that has anything to do with me going to this group. I think it is because my eyes are open now. Well maybe that is because of the Queen's Project."

"Whatever has happened to you Bobbi I am glad that you are sharing it with me."

"Girl, don't get all sentimental on me. You know I love you guys and I want us all to be better women and feel better about ourselves."

"I totally agree and I can't wait until I see you guys tonight."

"I can't wait either. So I have to go now and finish making myself beautiful for my date."

"See you tonight."

"See you later Colleen."

CHAPTER TWENTY EIGHT

Roberta

Colleen is so funny. I know she is going to change clothes and call Phillip. That is just how she is. She is so sweet and she never wants to make any one feel uncomfortable. So if he wants her to change she will. That's Colleen, pleasing until the end.

I know she is going to be so surprised when I tell her who I'm going to dinner with tonight. Amanda already knows and is happy for us. Not that we are a couple or anything. She's just happy that we decided to talk. She thinks Joe is wonderful and I am starting to agree with her. I never thought of him in any other way than just a guy who tries to talk to all of the women who come into the restaurant. I am pretty sure that I am not the only one who thinks that way. That's why I know Colleen is going to be so shocked when I tell her.

Every since he called me that night after I had dinner with my sisters we've been talking and enjoying each other's company. No sex involved yet, we are just spending time together getting to know each other and trying to weigh each other out. It's great and also surprising. I was so surprised when I picked up the phone that night when he first called me.

"Hello."

"Hello Bobbi, how are you?"

"I'm fine, who is this?"

"What you don't recognize my voice?"

"Please, I don't have time for games. Who is this?"

"This is Joe."

"Joe?"

"Yes."

"How did you get my number?"

"Does it matter?"

"At this point, and after the day I have had, no it doesn't really matter. So what's up Joe?"

"Nothing much, just thought I'd call and see if I could take you out for a drink tonight."

"No not tonight Joe. It has been a long day."

"Sorry to hear that. Is there anything I can do?"

"Can you place me in a new family?"

"Oh Bobbi don't say that. It can't be that bad."

"It's worst. Sometimes I wish I could just disappear and never talk to my family again."

"You don't mean that. Your family can't be all that bad."

"You don't know the half."

"Feel like talking about it . . . ."

That was our first conversation and it lasted three hours. I never knew Joe could be so sensitive and just so caring. I ended up telling him all about how my mother wanted me to go see my father before he dies.

I also told him about the person Marshall had been to my sisters and me. He shared a lot of important things about his life too. I now understand why he has dated so many women. He has never really met anyone who he really cared about. He stated that his father was a player also. He said he taught him all about the game. He grew up without a mother and was raised by his father. His mother died when he was ten and his father never remarried. But he did have a different woman everyday of the week. He had women who cooked for them and one who cleaned the house and washed their clothes. He said his father even had a woman who went to his school conferences. That was the only life he knew and if it worked for his father, he knew it would work for him. No woman has ever required him to be more than he is.

After listening to him for hours I could tell he had not met the right woman yet. I'm not saying I'm that woman, but one never knows.

Joe arrived right on time. And oh my goodness, this man is so smooth. He looks so good all dressed up in nice slacks and a black leather jacket. That silk blue shirt matched his skin color perfectly. That caramel light skin and that curly black hair, makes this man look good enough to eat. However we have not went that far yet. Don't get me wrong, I have thought about it over and over again, but we want it to be right. We don't want it to happen in a moment of weakness. We both stated that we have had those types of situations happen in the past one time too many.

"Wow Bobbi, you look so good!" He said while hugging me.

"Thank you Joe. You look good too. But of course you always look good."

"You're just saying that."

"No I'm not. You know you look good man. That's why all those women at the bar can't get enough of you."

"But I've had enough of them. I am only interested in one woman these days." He said and grabbed me in his arms. "Now this feels right."

"I have to agree Joe, it is surprisingly pleasant."

He then held me tighter and kissed me. I think I felt my knees buckle under me a little. If we didn't have dinner plans tonight and if I didn't have plans with my girls afterwards, I swear we would end up in bed tonight.

"I think we should stop before we miss dinner."

"I think you're absolutely right Joe. So let me grab my jacket and purse so we can go."

"I agree. I am kind of hungry."

"Are you hungry for food or hungry for something else?"

"Ok, now you better stop before we change our minds about dinner."

"You're right, let's go."

We left my place and headed to dinner. We had dinner at a very nice Mexican restaurant that I suggested. He said since I right reviews for restaurants for a living, he will trust me completely. I usually pick great places to eat and this time I did it again. He loved the food.

We ate dinner and made small talk. We both could tell that we were thinking about what almost happened earlier at my place, but we didn't say anything about it. We just ate our food and continued to stare at each other between bites.

After dinner we decided to ride together to Amanda's place. He said he had some inventory he needed to do while I hang with the girls. Afterwards he could give me a ride back to my place.

When we walked in, I saw Amanda sitting at our usual table talking with a waitress and one of her customers. She stood up when I walked over.

"Bobbi, give me a hug! I miss you so much." She said. I could tell she had already started drinking without us.

"I missed you too Amanda! What are you drinking? I want one too."

She told her waitress that was standing there to get me a Cosmo.

"Sit down Bobbi and tell me what has been going on?"

"Stop tripping Amanda, you just want to know what happened tonight with me and Joe."

"You're right Bobbi. I think this is so great!"

"What's so great?"

"What's great is the fact that we are all happy."

"Who's happy?" Colleen asked as she walked up to the table. And sure enough she had on a nice conservative pant suit. I knew her ass was going to change clothes.

"Sit down Colleen and let me order you a Cosmo."

"Good, I could use one."

Amanda summoned the same waitress and put up two fingers. The waitress shook her head so I know she knew what Amanda meant.

"Colleen you are dressed very nice."

"Shut-up Bobbi, you know that man has issues. Wait hold the fuck up! Amanda what is that on your finger?"

"Oh my God! Amanda I hadn't even noticed!"

"Ladies I'm getting married!" She yelled which made everyone in the restaurant turn and look at the three of us yelling and hugging.

"Amanda when did he ask you to marry him? Let me see that ring again." Colleen said.

"Wow that is probably the biggest ring I have ever seen. That has to be at least ten carrots."

"You are exactly right Bobbi. How did you know?"

"Girl as long as I have been window shopping for a ring, I should know exactly how many carrots that puppy is." I said and again we all started laughing.

The waitress walked over with our drinks.

"Amanda we are so happy for you!"

"I agree with Colleen. Nobody deserves it more than you Amanda. Let's make a toast to this wonderful occasion." I said.

"I agree."

We all lifted our glasses.

"To Amanda" I started. "God truly blessed us when you became a part of our lives. I am speaking for Colleen and myself. May God bless this union and keep you both happy and in love."

We all clicked glasses and took a sip of our drinks.

"So where are you guys going to live? Here or in Atlanta?"

"I don't know yet Colleen. We haven't talked about it yet. We haven't even set a date yet."

"There is just so much to do. I know you are going to make us both your bride maids."

"Of course she is Colleen. We wouldn't have it any other way. And Amanda I know a great wedding planner that could set your wedding off."

"That's great Bobbi. Get me her number and yes both of you guys are going to be in my wedding. You guys are my two best friends and I love you both. I just don't know what I am going to do if I can't see you guys every week."

"I was just thinking the same thing. Tell Hamilton that he is just going to have to move here." I said.

"I wish I could Bobbi, but most of his work is done there in Atlanta. But as Gladys Knight says, "I'd rather live in his world, than live without him in mine."

"I know that's right! I'll toast to that."

"Me too Colleen."

The rest of the evening was spent talking about the wedding and how happy we were for Amanda. I finally told Colleen who it was that I had been dating and how nice he really is. She seemed surprised but not shocked. She said that she could see us together and that we make a good couple. It seemed that all of us finally had some happiness to talk about. But the most wonderful part of the night was the fact that Amanda was happy and It seemed that after all the mess she had in dealing with her ex husband she finally will find some happiness.

However Colleen talked about how jealous and obsessive Phillip was becoming.

"Why do you think he is so jealous Colleen?"

"I don't know Amanda. I think it has something to do with the women in his past."

"Well he picked them so he should probably reevaluate what it is about him that made him want those types of women in the first place."

"You're right Bobbi. I think it had a lot to do with his low self esteem issues."

"I think he is probably just nervous about having a woman like you Colleen."

"What do you mean Bobbi?"

"I mean you're technically a celebrity around here. You're also beautiful and let you tell it, you have the bomb pussy?"

"Bobbi you are a fool." Colleen said while we all were laughing like school girls.

"Well ladies we have to cut this night off so I can get up and do some work tomorrow."

"Quit lying Colleen. You know you are running your ass over to see Phillip tonight."

"You're right Bobbi. I did tell him that I would be over when I left here."

"Where's Sabrina?"

"She's with my brother. It seems she has practically moved in with his family. She has her tail over there every weekend."

"It does seem that way." Amanda said.

"I don't bother her about it though. I figure she went a lot of years being disconnected from them and this is how she and my niece Novi are catching up."

"I think it is so nice that they are like sisters."

"I do too Bobbi." Colleen said and stood up.

"I am so glad we got a chance to hang out tonight. It seems we hardly see each other anymore." I said.

"Don't start Bobbi. We see how you keep looking over there in the direction of the bar."

"What are you talking about Colleen? I am just looking around."

"Looking around my ass! You can't seem to take your eyes off of Joe."

"That's not true Colleen. I'm just looking around."

"Whatever! Give me a hug ladies because I have to go now or I will never get out of here."

We all stood up and hugged each other. It felt kind of strange however. It seemed we stood there hugging much longer than we usually do.

"I love you guys." Colleen said.

"We love you too." Now go before that man of yours comes here to get you."

"You're right Bobbi. He is probably looking at the clock as we speak. Good night ladies."

Colleen left and Amanda and I continued to talk and laugh. We ended up talking for about another hour when Joe approached the table.

"Hate to break up this wonderful night, but I do believe that it is time to close the kitchen Amanda."

"I do believe you are right. I am going to take a peek in the kitchen because there are some things that I need to discuss with Chef before the night is done."

"Ok dear give me a hug and I will see you tomorrow at the Queen's Project." I said.

"Yes and I'm looking forward to it. I miss hanging with my girls so any chance I get I am going to take it. So goodbye and you too have a good night."

"You have a good night too Amanda. And again I'm so happy for you."

"Bobbi I am happy for you too." She said and pointed at Joe and walked away.

Joe and I left because he was my ride. This was the first time a man had ever cared enough to make sure I got home safe after a night of drinking with the girls. Not only did he drive me home, he even made sure I made it in safely.

"I really appreciate you driving me tonight Joe. That was really nice of you."

"It was my pleasure Bobbi. You don't have to thank me."

"Come on in and rest your coat. I can get you a glass of wine if you like. Oh I'm sorry, I didn't even ask if you were about to leave. It is pretty late."

"No, I am not in a hurry to leave, and yes I would love a glass of wine."

"Alright have a seat and I will be right back."

"I hope you like Merlot because that is all I have."

"Merlot is fine."

I went to my kitchen and poured him a glass of wine. When I walked back in my living room he had taken off his jacket and looked very comfortable sitting on my couch. We sat and listened to music and laughed and talked until around 3:00am.

"Oh my goodness I can't believe how late it is. I better be going I know you have to get up and head to the hospital to see your father. Are you nervous about seeing him?"

"Sort of, but I am not going tomorrow. I am going to wait for my sisters to pick a day to go. I will see them tomorrow and I am sure we will pick a day then to all go see him together. Truthfully, I hope they both change their minds and decide that seeing him is not a good idea. But if they don't change their minds I will go anyway. Even if I don't want to, I promised my sisters that I would go."

"Well I guess I better go. I have taken up way too much of your time as it is." He said and got up and headed to the door. "I just want to say thanks for a lovely evening Bobbi." He said and kissed me on the cheek.

"It was a great evening. I just hate it has to end." I said.

He put his arms around me and kissed me like I had never been kissed before. Man he had some soft lips. I instantly melted in his arms. I do believe I have never felt this hot from a kiss before. The next thing I knew he had picked me up and carried me to my room. I don't know how he figured out which room was my bedroom, but I am just glad he did.

We made love and when I say "made love" I mean it. I have never felt like I was truly being loved until this very moment. I know it sounds crazy, but this has to be the strangest thing that has ever happened to me. I was truly involved. I didn't care about the time or getting up early. All I knew was that this moment in time is what love making is all about. It is when two people completely lose themselves in each other. I am so glad that I can finally say, "Yes I am here."

CHAPTER TWENTY NINE

Amanda

We all decided to meet right outside of the hall where the meeting was to be held. I was there first because it wasn't that far from my ex-husband's house. So I was able to drop off the kids and head right over. There were so many cars in the lot that I had to park almost at the end of the lot. I didn't mind though.

When I made it into the building I decided to stand in the front so I could make myself visible to the girls when they showed up. Before long Colleen arrived. Looking like she just stepped out of a photo shot. Her makeup and hair was flawless. She was dressed in all white with gold accessories. Then Bobbi walked in with a glow on her face. She must have had a wonderful night with Joe. I am sure she will tell us later. Her sisters followed not long after so we all walked in together.

The place was so packed and the only seats were in a corner near the back. We wanted to all be able to sit together so we chose a small table that had five seats.

We made small talk until they introduced the facilitator. When she walked out everyone stood up and cheered. We all followed each other by standing and applauding. However, Bobbi cheered the loudest.

When she walked out, I noticed she had a smile that could light up a room. And her beauty was enchanting. She looked like she was a true Queen. She could easily charm anyone with those looks of hers.

She began her speech with a brief introduction of herself and her program. She talked about how she started "The Queen's Project" and why she started it. She talked about having self-awareness and the importance of recognizing who you are and where you come from.

She went on for over an hour and everyone in the room seemed to be holding on to her every word. They looked like they could hold on forever. I have to be honest, I was mesmerized also! Bobbi was right! This woman was powerful and a true gift from God. She talked about everything from relationships to being single and still feeling whole.

I could see why so many women come from near and far to hear her speak. But what brought me to tears was when she started talking about not being conscience while making decisions.

She stated:

"You know how a person can get a blow that literally knocks them out? Do you know how people sometimes say that we make a conscience decision to do things or we make conscience decisions to let people in our lives? Well I can remember a point in my life when none of my decisions were conscience ones. You see I had been hurt so bad in life that I was knocked out. I felt like I was sleeping through most of my life. I was making decisions and choosing people to be a part of my life while I wasn't conscience. Therefore, there is no way that any of those decisions were made by a person who was fully awake. See ladies, when the mind goes to sleep, so does your rational thinking. Sometimes we can be hurt so bad that we just close down and sleepwalk through life."

Everyone was clapping and on their feet including everyone at our table. Some of us must have been sleeping for years, including me. After that mess with my ex-husband, I just let life past me by. I would say to myself often whatever happened, happened.

She went on to say, "This has probably happened to lots of us. But think about it for a moment. If that pain would never have happened to you, then you would not have shut down or slept while making decisions. And if you weren't sleep or knocked out, then some of the bad decisions you made, maybe you would never have made them. These decisions made while you weren't conscience. It's like walking into a brick wall. Have you ever looked back and thought about some of the people you allowed in your life? Did you say to yourself, "What was I thinking?" See ladies, you weren't thinking and you weren't conscience. We don't make conscience decisions while we're sleeping. But think about this ladies, there will come a time when you have to wake up."

Screams and applauds throughout the room.

"See when you wake up, when you truly wake up, you look at these people and those decisions and you say to yourself, "What just happened?"

Everyone in the room must have known exactly what she was talking about because it was evident in the way the women in the room were yelling. What a dynamic and profound woman. I am so thankful that Bobbi introduced us to this group. I will be forever thankful to her.

The program ended just about an hour and a half after it started. Afterwards everyone was in the lobby buying her books and trying to get her autograph. I decided that I would try also. Bobbi was already standing in line waiting to get her book signed when I looked up.

"Bobbi, thank you so much for this. I have never been so touched by anyone in my whole life."

"I have to agree with Amanda." Colleen said. "She really made me open my eyes. I can't wait to hear her again."

"I am just glad you both enjoyed yourselves."

"We did. What about your sisters? I see they ran out as soon as it was over."

"Yeah they had to go pick up Sherry's twins from my mom's house. But they hugged me on their way out and said they enjoyed it."

"I have to leave too you guys. I have to meet Phillip for a late lunch. Can one of you purchase my book for me?"

"Don't worry Colleen, I'll get it. I was going to buy you and Amanda both a book."

"That's so sweet Bobbi. Are you sure?"

"Yes Colleen I'm sure. I know you have to go. Call us later."

"I will. I love you both and thank you again Bobbi for everything. You don't know how bad I needed this."

"Yes I do. Just as bad as I did." Bobbi said.

"Well ladies I have to go." Colleen said and hugged us both before leaving.

"Why is it 'that Colleen seems to always be running to meet Phillip? Why is he not running to meet her?"

"You're right Amanda. I hope Colleen was really listening to what she just heard in here. Because sometimes I think she is in over her head."

"Me too Bobbi. I wanted to ask you if you watched her news cast the other morning? Is it me, or did she look a little tired?"

"She did, but maybe she was just up all night"

"Bobbi you are so crazy! Speaking of up all night, what time did you get to sleep Ms. Thing?"

"I don't know what you're talking about Amanda."

"Don't play with me Bobbi! Tell me everything."

"Right here while we're standing in line?"

"I guess you're right. But let's go grab some coffee after we get these books signed."

"Ok Amanda, I'll tell you everything."

We waited another hour in that long line to get her autograph. It was worth it though because she was about to go on a book tour for a while and won't be doing any groups for almost a year. I am so glad I got in on this before she left. I owe Bobbi big time.

We ended up at our favorite coffee shop to talk. Bobbi knew I wasn't going to let her get away with not telling me everything.

We both ordered cappuccinos and sat in the back by a window.

"So tell me all the details."

"What details Amanda? What we should be discussing is your wedding plans."

"Stop fucking with me Bobbi, what happened with you and Joe after you guys left."

"He took me home and came in for a drink."

"That's it! Did he stay over?"

"Ok, the truth is that we had a wonderful night."

"Oh wow! I knew it Bobbi! I knew if you just gave him a chance he could be a good guy for you!"

"He is a good guy Amanda and I thank you for hooking us up."

"So is he a good lover?"

"I don't even know how to describe what happened last night. I truly think that last night I was making love to my soul mate."

"What? Was it like that?"

"Yes, I was transformed to another place Amanda. I have had good lovers in my time but never like this. No man has ever made me melt in their arms like he did."

"I am so happy for you guys Bobbi. That is exactly how I feel about Hamilton."

"Look at all of us Amanda. Just a few months ago none of us even thought love would show up again."

"Bobbi, are you saying that you're in love with Joe?"

"No, at least I don't think so. But one thing is for sure, I can see love on this journey."

"God is good."

"Yes He is Amanda."

CHAPTER THIRTY

Colleen

I could not wait to go to lunch with Phillip and tell him how great this woman was. He said he heard of her before but wasn't really interested in hearing any woman do any "man bashing". I will be glad to report that he has it all wrong. It is not about bashing anyone. It's about loving yourself and realizing that love starts with you!

I decided to stop by my house first to see if Sabrina and my niece Novi need anything. They made it to my house early this morning. That is how it is sometimes. Sabrina will say that she is staying the whole weekend away and then she will come home early. I think she is sort of like I am. I like to be out, but when it's time for sleep I like to be in my own bed.

Checking on the girls before I head over to Phillip's house is a must because I know once I get with him it could be hours before I get back home. That is how it is with us. Once we see each other, we just can't get enough of each other. It's like animal attraction. That's why I am glad that Novi is staying at our house with Sabrina tonight. That way she won't be waiting on me to get home. Last night they were at my brother's but they decided to hang out at my house tonight. I am truly glad that they are hanging out so much. I have not seen my daughter so happy in so long. She is always smiling and laughing which makes me smile and laugh too.

"Girls come down here!" I yelled as soon as I came through the garage door that leads to my kitchen. I had to yell because I could hear the music coming from upstairs.

They both came running.

"Yes mom? I thought you would be home later."

"I know that's what I said, but I thought I would stop by home to see if you guys were ok."

"We're ok Auntie." Novi said. "But we could use some money for pizza.

That was Novi. She never had a problem with speaking up. Just like her dad.

"Ok, here is a twenty." I reached in my purse and Novi was the first to grab it.

"Do you want us to save you some Mom?"

"No I am going to grab a bite with Phillip. I should be back in a few hours."

"Ok see you later and have fun Mom."

"You guys have fun too."

We hugged and I headed out the door. But soon as I got in my car my phone started ringing. It was Phillip.

"Hey baby."

"Colleen where are you?"

"I am just getting in my car."

"Are you just now leaving the event?"

"No I stopped by the house to check on the girls."

"I wish you would have called to tell me that you would be running late."

"I'm not late Phillip. I'll be right there. It shouldn't take me more than twenty minutes to get there."

"Whatever Colleen."

"What does that mean? Phillip is something wrong?"

"Yes there is something wrong Colleen. You have had me waiting for over an hour and now you still expect me to wait longer."

"I don't think it's been over an hour Phillip."

"Yes it has Colleen and I think you are being inconsiderate!"

"Phillip calm down. I'll be there in a few."

"Bye Colleen." He said and hung up.

I don't know what has gotten into Phillip lately. He has really been having serious mood swings. It seems like every other day it's something with him. He is acting so jealous too. He has to believe that I want him and only him. He should know that after I changed clothes for him last night and then went back to his house with nothing but my coat on. When I walked in and took off my coat, I asked him if he liked my birthday suit better. He hugged me and we made crazy love for over two hours. And when I say crazy love, I mean we were knocking over furniture and tables, pulling hair and biting each other. Hell my body is still hurting from that session.

I made it to Phillip's house in about fifteen minutes. The door was open when I walked up.

"Why are you sitting in here in the dark with the door opened Phillip?"

"I'm just waiting on you."

"Ok, I'm here. Let's go eat."

"Sit down Colleen first so we can talk."

"Talk about what Phillip?" I said and sat on the couch next to him.

"We need to talk about us."

"What about us? Phillip I thought we were fine."

"I thought we were fine too until today."

"What happened today?"

"You showed me just how much you really care about us today."

"What are you talking about Phillip? I didn't do anything today."

"You left me waiting while you hung out with whomever, after lying about hanging with your friends. Did you really even go to any event?"

"What are you talking about Phillip? You know I was with my friends at the Queen's Project event. I told you I was going so I don't understand where you're going with this."

"If that's the case then why did you have to go home first? What did you have to do? Go home and shower before you get over here to me?"

"You can't be serious Phillip! How can you say such things after the night we just spent?"

"That's the same thing I was thinking. How can you be with another man after the night we had?"

"Phillip sometimes I don't believe you know me at all. I am not that type of woman." I said yelling.

"Why are you getting so upset Colleen? Is it because I touched a nerve? The truth comes out and you can't take it. I guess you can't take me seeing your true colors. I hate women like you."

"I can't believe I'm having this conversation with you. How dare you accuse me of such maliciousness! I am out of here!" I said and headed to the door. "I'll get my shit later."

"Colleen can you wait and tell me why you are leaving? We can work this out if you agree to never see this other man again."

"Goodbye Phillip. And for the record I was totally content with only you. There is no other man. But you know what man you remind me of right now, my deceased husband!" I said and stormed out of his house.

I can't believe this man! How can he be so insecure? He reminded me of some of the things that my husband used to say to me right before he would beat the shit out of me for stuff I never did. I can't deal with another crazy abusive man. I can't and won't go through this shit again with any man! And the bad part about it is that I really like Phillip. I thought he was different. I could even see me being with him for the rest of my life.

But I guess when it is all said and done, none of these men know how to treat their women like Queens. However Phillip is a good man when he is not tripping. Fuck! Those other women in his past really messed him up.

CHAPTER THIRTY ONE

Roberta

"I should be there in about an hour Mama."

"An hour? Your sisters are headed to the hospital right now."

"Really, then I will try and hurry. I will leave my office in about twenty minutes. Can you call Dottie and tell her to wait on me before they go in?"

"Tell me why Roberta?"

"Because Mama I don't want to walk in his room by myself. What if his wife and other kids are there?"

"You are being silly honey. You have every right to be there. You are his child too."

"I know Mama, but it's still a little uncomfortable to be there with his other family."

"I understand baby so I will call Dottie and Sherry and tell them to wait on you."

"Thanks Mama."

"The girls told me that they really enjoyed that woman's group that you all attended."

"Yes that's what they said. That was a couple of weeks ago and I haven't heard from them since."

"I know you haven't. Sherry went to that conference last week in Texas while Dottie kept the boys."

"Oh yeah, I remember she told me she was going away."

"They also told me about the new guy in your life."

"What new guy?"

"You know what new guy I'm talking about. I'm talking about the one that you have been spending all of your spare time with."

"It's not like that Mama. He's just a friend right now."

"That's fine honey. I want you to find love and happiness. Don't end up like me."

"What do you mean Mama? There is nothing wrong with you."

"I just don't want you to waste your life waiting on something to happen. I want you to find happiness and live."

"Mama are you saying that you didn't live your life? I remember when you used to go out and party and have dates all the time. It looked to me like you had a lot of fun back then."

"It just seemed that way dear. I was just trying to keep busy so I could take my mind off all of my worries."

"What were you worried about Mama?"

"Baby I worried about a lot of things."

"Things like what Mama?"

"I worried about if Marshall was coming to see us and when."

"Really, you were worried about that?"

"Yes I was worried about that all the time. I loved him so much that I couldn't help but think about him?"

"Mama, can I ask you a question?"

"Of course you can ask me anything."

"Why did you have children with a married man?"

"I just told you that I loved him."

"But you knew that he was married and that you couldn't have him."

"Is that what has been bothering you for all these years Roberta, the fact that your father was married?"

"Yes and the fact that he has never been there for us. He missed everything Mama. He was never someone we could talk to about our problems or anything that was going on in our lives. He wasn't there to walk Dottie down the aisle when she got married. He has never spent any time with Sherry's twins. Hell he probably doesn't even know their names. How were we ever to know that we were Queens if our own father didn't think so? Then of course we wouldn't look for men to treat us like that either."

"Roberta sometimes life can be so confusing. You never know who you're going to love and why you will love them. I never meant to love Marshall and I'm sure he never meant to love me either."

"So you think he loved you Mama?"

"I don't think it Roberta, I know it. Like I said before honey, love can be confusing."

"I guess. Look Mama I have to go, I will call you later."

"Alright baby, you hurry and get to that hospital."

"I will Mama. I love you."

"I love you too baby."

Damn! Just when I think my mother is going to give me some profound words of wisdom, all she can think of to say is that love is confusing. That doesn't work for me. I already know that. I just wanted to know why it has to be.

I made it to the hospital in about forty-five minutes. When I got to the third floor where Marshall's room was, I headed in the direction of room 316. I knew his room number by heart from the numerous times my mother said it.

While walking down the hallway I almost passed the waiting room. Dottie and Sherry were sitting there looking worried.

"Hey what's up?"

"Nothing Bobbi." Dottie said and got up and hugged me. Sherry did the same.

"So glad you made it in time."

"In time for what Sherry. Is visiting hours almost over?"

"No Bobbi, Marshall is dying. His wife just told us that the doctor said he probably won't make it through the end of the day."

I stood there without blinking, but I couldn't understand why. Why should I care if this man lives or dies? He never cared about me.

"We told his wife and their children that we would wait here until you arrived. I told her we all wanted to walk in together." Dottie said.

"That's fine Dottie. Let's just go in."

"Are you sure you're ready Bobbi? We can take a moment to breathe if you want."

"No I'm fine. I'm ready to do this."

The three of us locked hands and walked in room 316. When we walked in his wife stood up and walked over to us. She hugged each one of us really hard. What was going on? I thought she hated us.

"He's been waiting for you guys." She said. "Go over to your father."

We walked over to the bed where Marshall was laying. His other children were there also. And to my surprise, they all smiled at us. Now I was really confused. Marshall opened his eyes as if he knew we were there.

"Hello." Dottie said to him with tears running down her face. He reached for her hand.

"Hey sunshine." He said very softly.

"Hey you, how are you doing?"

"Baby I'm ok now. No pain at all and where's your sisters?"

"They are here."

"Hello Marshall." I said.

"Hey Marshall." Sherry said.

"I am the happiest man around. I have all of my children together in the same room. I just want you three to know that I love you and I am sorry for letting you down. I never meant for any of this to happen." He said and started coughing.

"No more talking, you need your rest." Dottie said.

"I am ok baby. I just need to say this. I have always wished for nothing but happiness for you. I am just sorry that I have been the one who caused you guys the most pain. But one thing for sure, I love you all. But love can be confusing and there are some things you can't understand. You three have always been my little Queens and I am sorry I never showed you or said that to you before now." He said and closed his eyes.

Marshall died right then and there. With all of the people he loved around him. All expect the one woman he really loved. I guess my mother was right.

Marshall's funeral was held the following week. There were so many people there including our mother. It seemed Marshall had lots of family that my mother knew. So many of them walked up to us and hugged us. Some even left their numbers. It is a crying shame for families to first meet at a funeral. But that is what happens when there are secrets in families.

It was a beautiful funeral and his wife and their children made sure all of us were involved in the planning. Truth be told, she was a very nice lady. She and my mother even hugged and held hands for a moment. His family did everything to make us feel like we were all a part of the family. The way it should have been in the first place.

CHAPTER THIRTY TWO

Colleen

It has been almost two months since I left Phillip's house mad that night. I still can't believe how angry he made me. I still don't care if I ever talk to him again. Well at least that's what I keep telling myself. It has been so hard not seeing him and spending time with him. It's so hard getting use to someone and then all of a sudden they are not in your life. Yes, Phillip had some crazy ways but deep down inside he's a good person. He's kind and he has a good heart. I think that he has been treated so badly in the past, that he can't tell when he has a good woman in his corner. His trust issues will always be a problem with anyone he ends up with.

What has been helping me the most with this break up is the fact that we have been planning Amanda's wedding. We all went to Bobbi's father's funeral, but after that we have been planning this wedding nonstop. I almost forgot how much fun planning a wedding truly is. I am so glad that she decided that she wanted to do the planning herself.

Amanda flew to Atlanta a couple of weeks ago and she and Hamilton set a date for their wedding. They picked December twenty third because they wanted a Christmas theme wedding. I have never heard of such a theme, but it is a first time for everything. The way Amanda has it planned and the decorations she has ordered, I can tell it is going to be the talk of all of her friends and family. Amanda has incredible taste and she knows what looks good. At one point I thought that one day I would be calling her to plan my wedding. Hell Phillip and I even laid in bed a few times talking about getting married. Maybe it just wasn't meant to be.

None the less, it's Friday and once again I get to hang with my girls. But first I have to take Sabina shopping for school supplies. Last week we shopped for clothes and had such a great time. She is growing up so fast and is truly becoming a young woman. She is looking forward to finishing up high school and heading to college where she will be majoring in journalism. What else.

Sabrina and I decided to start at the mall so that way we could do most of the shopping there and not run all around for her supplies. I have a funny feeling that she just wanted to go to the mall again. She says it's because I have been running around like a chicken with my head cut off. (Not that she would know what that looks like. She picked that saying up from me.)

Maybe I have been trying to do a lot lately. It does seem like there is never enough time in the day to do all the things I need to get done. I think I am just trying to keep busy. If I sit still I will think of Phillip and this huge need I have to hear his voice or to have his arms wrapped around me. There have been some nights when I have cried myself to sleep. I wish I could move on from this.

However hard this may be, I still have to see his sister every morning when I go to work. She always has something nice to say. She thinks that her brother made the worst mistake by letting me go. She also said that she thinks he knows he messed up because lately he has been really depressed and keeping to himself. She said that his ex-wife has been the one keeping the kids most of the time. I feel bad for him but I'm not reaching out to him. He has to get help first before I talk to him again.

Sabrina and I made it to the mall around two. She had a whole list of things she needed for school. I never knew being a junior in high school was so demanding.

"Mom let's get another piercing in our ears."

"Sabrina I can't do that."

"Why, because of your job?"

"That's one reason."

"What are the other reasons?"

"I just don't want to get my ears pierced again. But you can if you'd like."

"No I want us to do it together."

"Well Sabrina you are going to have to think of something else we can do together."

"What about a tattoo?"

"You're too young for a tattoo."

"I'm not talking about today Mom. I'm talking about when I graduate."

"I'll think about it."

"No don't think about it Mom. Let's just agree to do it."

"Sabrina, tell me why do you have this sudden interest in doing something together? It's usually that you want to spend all your time with Novi. Is something going on with you guys?"

"Of course not Mom I love hanging with them. In fact, I was wondering if you could drop me off when we leave here."

"Then tell me why the urgency to do something with me?"

"I just think that you have been sad lately since the break up with Phillip. I just want you to know that you will always have me."

"Sabrina you are the sweetest person I know." I said and hugged her tight.

"I know Mom. You are sweet too. So what about the tattoo? Are we going to get one?"

"What kind of tattoo?"

"I was thinking about getting maybe small butterflies on our backs."

"That might be nice. Let me think about it."

"Well you have a little over a year to decide."

"Good that gives me plenty of time."

We finished shopping and headed out of the mall. A simple trip for school supplies ended up costing me around three hundred dollars. This girl sure can spend money.

Just as we were getting in the car my cell phone rang. I reached in my purse to grab it and saw that it was Phillip's number. I pushed ignore on my phone and dropped it back in my purse. The nerve of his ass waiting so long to call me! I wanted to talk to him and tell him off but not in front of Sabrina.

"Who was that?"

"Nobody, get in the car so we can get home and I can get myself ready for a night with the girls."

"Are you still going to drop me off?"

"Yes on my way out."

As soon as we walked in the house my cell phone was ringing again. I hurried into my bedroom to answer it this time. It was Phillip again.

"Hello."

"Hello Colleen."

"Hello Phillip, what do you want?"

"I need to talk to you. Do you have time to talk and hear me out?"

"You can't be serious Phillip. Why has it taken you over two months to call me?"

"I have just been going through some things Colleen. I needed time to get my head on straight."

"What are you talking about Phillip? I don't understand any of this. Why are you calling me?"

"I am calling you because I need to see you. I need to talk to you face to face about everything. Colleen I love you and I need to tell you how much."

"I don't need to hear that you love me Phillip. Loving me is not the problem we had. The problem was you not trusting me."

"I know I was wrong Colleen. I was crazy and I couldn't see straight. I have never had a woman like you. I was just so insecure. I always thought you would find someone better and leave me."

"But I never gave you a reason to be insecure Phillip. I was only into you and I tried to tell you that but you wouldn't listen."

"I know Colleen. I was stupid and I am sorry. Please forgive me and say that you will see me."

"I can't do that Phillip. I have plans tonight and I am not going to change them."

"Plans with who?"

"That's none of your business."

"You're right Colleen. I have no right to ask you any questions. All I ask is that you consider seeing me after your plans tonight."

"Phillip I can't. I'm not ready for that and I don't know if I ever will be."

"Please, please Colleen." He said sounding as if he was crying. "Please just let me talk to you."

"Phillip I have to go so I can get dressed."

"Will you call me if you change your mind?"

"I won't change my mind Phillip. Goodbye." I said and hung up. He must be out of his mind. He thinks he can sound sad and I would just take him back. I miss him like crazy but I can't go through that again. I need to be strong and just concentrate on something else.

My something else was a night with the girls drinking, laughing and talking shit like we always do.

I got dressed and dropped Sabrina off at my brother's house on my way to the restaurant. When I walked in, I saw Bobbi sitting at the bar talking to Joe. I have to admit, they sure do look good together and it seems that Bobbi is a whole different person lately. I walked over to the bar where they both were.

"Hello love birds."

"Hello Colleen." Bobbi said as we hugged.

"Hello Colleen, what can I get you?"

"Hello Joe, you can get me the usual."

"Alright, one Cosmo coming up."

"How are you dear? You are looking amazing as usual."

"Thanks Bobbi so are you." I said. Truth is Bobbi has this amazing glow on her face every since her father Marshall died. The fact that he said he has always loved them did wonders for her. It seems she is more open to love now. Isn't it strange how the love of a parent can change how you look at life? I am happy for her.

"I may look amazing but it has been a long week girl. I need this weekend so bad."

"What happened Bobbi?"

"It's just that work is getting crazy and I need to find a new job."

"Really, I thought you loved writing the articles and being the food critic for the paper."

"I do love it but I can't say it's my dream job. It pays the bills is all I can say. So what's going on with you? How was shopping with Sabrina? Did she spend all of your money?"

"Yes she did. That girl really knows how to shop. But guess who called as soon as we left the mall?"

"Who?"

"Phillip?"

"Really, hurry Joe and pass that Cosmo to Colleen." Bobbi said. Joe was just finishing pouring it into a glass.

"Come on Bobbi, let's get to our table."

"Okay Joe keep them coming." Bobbi said and kissed him before we walked away.

"So sit and tell me all about your phone call Colleen."

"You mean calls. He has now called me a total of six times."

"No shit! What is he saying?"

"He's trying to play on my sensitive side. He's acting like he's crying."

"Maybe he is. Why do you think he's acting?"

"He wants me to stop what I'm doing and run to him."

"Tell the truth Colleen, a part of you wants to be in his arms right now."

"You are so right Bobbi, but I can't let him know that."

"Know what?" Amanda asked as she walked up to the table and sat down.

"We are talking about the calls Colleen has got from Phillip."

"Really, what does he want?"

"He is trying to get me to come over to his house and listen to him beg me to come back to him."

"You know you want to Colleen. You should go and hear him out and still leave after you let him beg you for about an hour."

"I don't think so Bobbi. I think Colleen is right about this. I agree she should give it more time. Meet him at a coffee shop or a place like that. That way if he is serious, he will cry right there in front of everyone." Amanda said and we all started laughing. We don't know any man that would cry in public around a bunch of strangers.

She was right though. Phillip needs to have some time to think about all of this. He can't believe that just because he wants me back I have to stop what I'm doing and run to him.

We sat there for hours drinking and laughing. We managed to get some wedding business done also. We picked the colors for more flowers and it was so nice that she wanted our input on everything. Amanda is going to make a lovely bride.

By eleven o'clock we were all full and could not drink another drink. It was getting late and time for all of us to call it a night.

"I am going to have to head home now. I need to get some rest." I said.

"Yes go home and get some sleep." Amanda said. "And thank you both for all of your help. I could not do this without you guys."

"You don't have to thank us Amanda. We love you and will do anything for you."

"Thanks Colleen. I love you both too."

"Are you leaving too Bobbi."

"Yes Amanda, I need to head home. I have to get up early and meet my mom and sisters for breakfast."

"What, no Joe tonight?"

"I never said that Colleen. I will see him when he gets off tonight."

"It's so nice to know that you two have love, and that you both are happy."

"You will find love again Colleen. You just have to wait on it. Real love for you too is out there. You just have to be patient."

"I know you are right Amanda but I am still lonely."

"I know you're lonely. But it won't always be like that."

"I believe you Amanda and I love your optimism." I said and we hugged.

Bobbi and I grabbed our bags and walked out the door to the back parking lot.

"I agree with Amanda Colleen. You are a great person and real love will come one day. It's probably not Phillip though. He stresses you too much and he needs to get his issues together before he can have a real relationship with anyone."

"You are right Bobbi and I totally agree. He is not the one. He does need to work on his problems first."

"Exactly, so give me a hug and call me tomorrow."

"I will. I love you Bobbi and thanks for being my sister."

We hugged and walked toward our cars. We turned and waved at each other before driving off.

As soon as I got home my phone started ringing again. It was Phillip. What is his problem? He has called around twenty times tonight. I decided to answer it this time.

"Phillip you have to stop this! You can't keep calling me like this!" I yelled into the phone.

"Then talk to me Colleen! I just need to talk to you face to face."

"Why do you need to see me Phillip? I will talk to you over the phone. I am not coming to your house."

"Please Colleen, just sleep on it and come in the morning."

"Let me think about it Phillip."

"If you say yes, I promise I won't bug you again. If after hearing what I have to say, you still want to leave, then I will understand."

"I'll call you tomorrow."

"Thank you Colleen."

"Good night Phillip."

I took a shower and thought a lot about what the girls said tonight. Love will come if I'm patient. But I guess that's easy for them to say, they both have someone to spend the rest of their life with. Amanda is getting married and Bobbi will probably be doing the same soon. I thought I would be next to walk down the aisle with my Mr. Right. I also thought Phillip could be Mr. Right. I thought a lot about Phillip. He sounded so pitiful. He really does love me and he probably just needs to know that I still love him, which I do.

I made it to Phillip's house by nine o'clock the next morning. I don't know what possessed me to go over there and listen to him. I just felt sorry for him and besides it won't hurt to give him about thirty minutes and then I'm out."

I knocked a couple of times before he answered. He opened the door but it didn't look like Phillip. He needed a haircut and a shave. He looked like he hadn't slept in days. I walked in.

"Phillip what's going on here? You haven't cleaned this place or yourself. You knew I was coming and you didn't even bother to straighten up the place."

"I don't feel good Colleen. In fact I haven't felt good in a long time. It's been ever since you left me for someone else."

"What did you say Phillip?"

"You heard me. I said ever since you left me for some other man."

"Is that why you wanted me to come over here? So you can keep accusing me of this shit. I'm out of here!"

"Don't move. Or I promise you, you'll be sorry."

"And what is that supposed to mean Phillip?"

"Just like I said Colleen." He said and reached under his couch pillow and pulled out a gun.

"Oh my God! Phillip what are you doing? I came here to listen to you! Please put that gun down! You are making me nervous! Please put that gun down Phillip!"

"No sit down Colleen! I want you to sit down and tell me the truth!"

"I am telling you the truth! Phillip nothing happened, it's all in your head!"

"Now you're calling me crazy?"

"No, no Phillip, that's not what I'm saying. Please just let me leave and we can talk about this later!"

"Hell no! Now Colleen sit down before you make me mad! I'm not going to tell you again." He said.

I sat down on the edge of his couch.

"Why are you doing this Phillip? I thought we were special. Why are you saying all of this stuff to me?"

"Because Colleen you are just like that bitch I married. She always had to have a man on the side."

"What are you talking about? I am not seeing anyone!"

"What about your plans you had last night with a man?"

"Phillip I was with my friends Amanda and Bobbi. Remember we always get together at Amanda's restaurant on Friday nights."

"Stop lying Colleen! I am getting so fucking tired of this!"

"Phillip put the gun down so we can talk calmly!"

"We are talking calmly. I'm just tired of all of this shit!"

"What shit Phillip? Put the gun down so we can talk."

"I'm sorry Colleen. I can't do that."

A neighbor heard gunshots and called the police. They found two bodies.

CHAPTER THIRTY THREE

Roberta

Today is the saddest day of my life. Today we are burying our best friend. Colleen was killed a few days ago by Phillip. It seems he just didn't want to live without her. Somehow he tricked her into coming to his house. I guess I kind of knew she was going to see him and I knew she was feeling lonely and I didn't do anything about it. I just wish there was something that I could have said to her to save her life. I will beat myself up about this for the rest of my life.

Hamilton flew in as soon as Amanda called him with the news and he hasn't left her side yet. He even told Amanda that it would be okay to postpone the wedding if she wanted to. Amanda quickly disagreed. She said that Colleen would never want her to do that. We both knew that Colleen really loved weddings and was looking forward to this one.

Joe has also been wonderful. He was lying next to me when Amanda called me that morning with the news. I could hardly understand what she was saying on the phone so Joe took the phone and talked to her.

She told him that Colleen's brother had just called her and told her that the police came to his house to tell him that Colleen was found dead in Phillip's house. I will never forget that day. How will we ever move on from this point? How does anyone?

And then there is Sabrina. My heart is aching for her. How is she going to make it without Colleen? They had become so close in recent months and I know she is taking this so hard. I am so glad she has her uncle with her, even though he is having a tough time also. We talked to them both to let them know that we will always be here if they ever need us.

Amanda closed the restaurant for the week, but will open it back for dinner after the funeral. Her staff has all volunteered to work and help out in any way they can. In fact the whole town is doing something to help Colleen's family get through this tragic time. Her news station had a very touching segment on her the other morning. They were all in tears and it made us all cry too. She was loved by so many people.

Her brother said that Sabrina will be staying with them and he wanted us to have the number so we can stay in touch with her. That is exactly what we wanted to hear. We both said that we would like to spend time with her when she is ready. We want to keep her close to us so she can always be able to ask questions about her mother. We know that we can't replace her mother, but we just want her to know that we are here for her.

We arrived at the church early for the family hour. I've never seen so many reporters and news cameras in one place in all my life. Colleen was a real superstar here. Her death has done something to our community and has brought us together in a way that is so powerful. It seems the whole town came out to say goodbye to their superstar and say how sorry they were for her family. When there is a senseless death it seems to bring out all types of caring people. Someone even called Amanda asking if she and I would speak about Colleen's death at a domestic abuse program. We don't know how or why they would call us, but Amanda told them that we would get back with them. That is how Amanda is, she is never rude. I would have probably cussed them out and told them not to ever call me again.

I didn't think I could walk into the church when we walked up to the door. But luckily Joe was right there holding my arm. My sisters and my mother were also there. Colleen's brother wanted us to sit with the family up front so we sat right behind them.

Colleen looked beautiful lying there. She was dressed in all white and she looked like she was sleeping. The funeral home did an excellent job on her. She looked very peaceful. Shana did her makeup and hair. No one was angry with Shana or her family. We realized that her brother's actions had nothing to do with her or her mother.

The family hour seemed more like family hours. Sabrina had to be taken out of the service twice and so did Amanda. Hamilton asked me to go to the restroom and check on her after she hadn't come back in a while. When I walked in Amanda grabbed me and we both hugged and cried on each other's shoulders.

"What happened Bobbi? Why did we let her go?" Amanda asked.

"I have been going over it in my mind. Why didn't we see the signs? How did he fool all of us for so long? I miss her so much Amanda. I don't think I can make it through this."

"Bobbi we have to make it through this. We just have each other now. Colleen would want us to be there for each other."

"I know she would. And I know we have to be strong for Sabrina. She can't see us lose it or she will break down again."

"It's so hard to look at her Bobbi. I don't know what is going to happen to her after this. I am so worried that she is going to lose her mind without Colleen."

"We have to pray for her Amanda. We have to pray every day and very hard. No child should have to go through such a horrible tragedy. She is just so young."

"I agree Bobbi." Amanda said and hugged me again. "Let's get back out there before she thinks we left."

We cleaned our faces and walked out of the restroom. Joe and Hamilton were standing by the door. They hugged us as we walked back into the sanctuary and returned to our seats. When we walked back in we could see that Sabrina and Novi was standing at the casket hugging. That is an image that will last in my mind forever.

It was a long service and a very nice one. There was not a dry eye in the house. It was a beautiful service and it was done with elegance and class. Just like Colleen. She was a very elegant woman and this is how she should have been received to the Lord. The pastor said so many wonderful things about Colleen. Her brother also talked about growing up with his baby sister. I have never heard such kind words in my life. Colleen would have been pleased.

After the service we all headed to the cemetery to say our final goodbyes. The station paid for all the funeral expenses and even bought the headstone. Driving to that place made me think of Marshall. It hadn't even been three months since he died. I didn't think that I would have to do this again so soon. I never thought that I would be burying one of my best friends.

We all made our way back to Amanda's restaurant for dinner. The place was packed. All the tables were done with white linen with white flowers and candles on each of them. Amanda's staff did a wonderful job with the place. People were everywhere talking and mingling. Sabrina stayed close to her uncle, but to my dismay she seemed to be coping good with everyone around. I even saw her smile a couple of times.

I didn't feel much like eating even with all the wonderful food that was there. Amanda had everything from fried chicken, roast, smothered pork chops, turkey and dressing, and everything else that goes with it. She had five different kinds of cakes and twelve different pies. There were salads and all kinds of breads. People were eating like they never ate before. Even my family was eating like crazy. My mother finally got a chance to give Joe the third degree about our relationship while sitting at the table with him. He laughed and seemed to really like my family. My mother sure likes him because she couldn't stop talking to him all evening. It was a truly nice dinner and Colleen's family was very appreciative. They kept thanking us for everything. It was Amanda who planned the dinner.

The night ended with hugs and everyone saying very nice things to Sabrina. We hugged Sabrina and she said she would call us soon. I hope so because it would be so nice to spend some time with her.

Amanda's staff stayed to clean up the restaurant. Joe and I asked if she wanted us to stay longer, but she insisted that we go home and get some rest. We said our goodbyes and I got in the car with Joe. We rode to my house in silence and I looked out of the window at the rain all the way. I couldn't help but think about Sabrina and what her life will be like from now on. My mother wasn't the best mother, but I don't know what I would have done without her. I don't know what any of us would have done without her. Sabrina has one hell of a journey ahead of her. None of our lives will ever be the same from here on out. Amanda is probably thinking the same thing right about now. Where do we go from here?

CHAPTER THIRTY FOUR

Amanda

It has been four months since Colleen was killed and now I'm getting married and moving to Atlanta. Hamilton and I decided that a move would be good for me. We found a nice house not far from his office and not far from a great school for the kids. It is a little larger than the house he already has there because we thought we would need more room with the kids there. It all worked out great too. His oldest son and his family are going to move into his old house that way they can keep the house in the family. We are all looking forward to a new start and a new adventure. My kids included. They are looking forward to the move and can't wait to start their new school. My ex-husband is even okay with the move as long as he gets the kids for the summer and some holidays. He loves his kids but he also knows that being with me the majority of the time is best for them.

My wedding was filled with so many different emotions. Bobbi and I were happy, but we cried the night before for hours while thinking and talking about

Colleen. We had a sleep over at my house just the two of us and we got so drunk. We were supposed to have a night of partying but it ended up being a night of tears and sadness. We both talked about how much we missed Colleen and how we wished we could have had more time with her. We still don't understand how someone could just take the life of such a wonderful kind person. She was so full of life and had so much to live for. No one saw this coming and no one really understands what happened. Even though a few weeks after the funeral, Shana told us what Phillip's ex-wife said about the abuse she suffered while with him. There were times when he would lock her in the house and threaten her while he had a gun in his hand. He would also beat her on occasions when no one was around. Shana said she didn't know this but found out later and told Colleen not long before she died. Again, another woman who was ashamed of the abuse that she endured while married to a man that everyone thought was perfect.

That is how it is so often. So many women are abused and are afraid to tell anyone or seek some help. Some are afraid of what people will say about them and others are afraid of what could happen to them if they were to tell anyone. I didn't tell anyone about the mental abuse I endured with my ex-husband because I was ashamed. Bobbi never told anyone because she was angry at herself most of the time for accepting it. And I am sure that Colleen thought that if she was nice and went along with what her husband was saying and doing, he would stop beating her. He never stopped beating her and telling her she was nothing. But abuse is abuse.

Looking back and thinking about everything Colleen said about why she stayed so long, I have come to the conclusion that it had a lot to do with the type of father she had. She came from a long line of men who abused women. Just like I come from a long line of men who cheat on their wife's and Bobbi was used to men like her father. Her father was the type of man who told lies and never showed her any love. Having these types of men in our lives has been the reason why we chose the men that we did. It is so hard to expect a man to treat you like a Queen when your own father didn't. I have learned that it is so important for women to have positive men in their lives. They as fathers are supposed to show their daughters what to look for in a man and what not to accept.

The wedding and reception was held at an elegant five star hotel downtown. We chose this hotel because it was in the heart of the city and our out of town guest could take in the sights of the city. We also chose to have the reception at the same place because it would be easier for us not to have our guest traveling in all of this snow and cold weather.

My dress was vanilla and trimmed with white beads. My bridesmaid's dresses were a soft winter white. Bobbi and Sabrina made such beautiful bridesmaids. Sabrina decided to stand in for her mother. I didn't even have to ask her to do it. She called me and asked if it would be okay because she knew that her mother was looking forward to being in my wedding. I could hardly talk when I heard her, but in between tears I said yes and I would love to have her stand in for her mother. She could not have given me a more perfect wedding gift. The only down to this day is the fact that I am leaving Bobbi. I know she will be alright though. She and Joe are tighter than ever. And since the facilitator of the Queen's Project is done touring, she has started back going to the group again. However, we will see each other often. Joe is taking over complete management of the restaurant so for now I will be back in town at least twice a month.

After the wedding and reception, Hamilton and I said our goodnights and headed to our honeymoon suite. We leave tomorrow for Aruba and will be there for ten days. After that we will be back in town to start packing up my stuff. I sold my house right away. A young couple put an offer in on the house two days after it went on the market. I figure if they were that anxious then it must be meant to be. They are a lovely couple and are expecting their first child. It is nice to know that there will be a family starting out their lives together in my house.

This has been a wonderful day and a wonderful wedding. As I look at my new husband and I think to myself that I am truly blessed. I never would have thought in a million years that I would end up with such a wonderful man. He makes my life complete and he has made me believe in love again. I now believe in real love and that there is love out there for anyone who believes. I thank God for him and I am looking forward to our future together.

FINAL CHAPTER

Roberta

"Doctor, I finally figured out why I was so mad all the time! I have finally realized where all of that anger came from. I was angry with my father for most of my life."

"And why were you angry with your father Roberta?"

"I was angry because he was not the man he should have been for me and my sisters. He being absent in my life, made me make some very bad choices in my life. My friends had the same issues because of their fathers. And I keep telling you doctor, please call me Bobbi."

"Okay Bobbi, what choices are you talking about?"

"The choices I made in the men I have been with."

"Are you saying that because of your father's absence you were not able to be with a decent man?"

"Well first of all, I have been looking back on all the men that I have dated in my thirty-five years. Most of them have been losers and never really treated me right."

"Go on."

"I have been thinking about this ever since I started attending a support group."

"What kind of a support group is this Bobbi? I hope it is not a man-bashing group."

"Dr. Lori, you know me better than that. I would not be in a group that had a bunch of women talking about the wrongs that men do. You should know how I am after all these sessions."

"Yes Bobbi, I know you are not the type of person that would sit through that type of group. Please go on and tell me more about this group."

"Okay, you remember me telling you about my two friends Amanda and Colleen?"

"Yes very well."

"Well someone told me about this group which at first I was a little skeptical, but I went and it changed my life completely. At first I never thought much about myself or even thought about what type of man I wanted to share my life with. But one day I opened my eyes and now I am able to say what I will accept and what I won't accept in a relationship."

"That is good to hear Bobbi. I am very pleased to know that there was a safe place that you could go for support."

"Yes Dr. Lori I am glad too."

"So Roberta, I mean Bobbi has any of this changed your mind about being angry with your father? It seems that you have learned different meanings of love. Are you still dealing with the death of your friend Colleen?

"Of course Doctor I am still dealing with it. How do I ever stop? And yes I am still angry about it too. But like I said before, I was angry about a lot of different things in my life. I just hate that she didn't get a chance to really figure out what it means to love and respect yourself."

"Are you saying that she didn't love herself?"

"Sometimes I feel that way. I feel that way because I believe if she could have loved herself more than these no good men that were in her life, and if she would have known real love in her life before Phillip came along, she may have been able to walk away from him."

"Has going to your group helped you deal with her death?"

"The Queen's Project taught me so much about myself and about loving myself. I will never forget the things I heard there and the way the facilitator presented them to us. I can honestly say that now I love myself and I have someone who loves me also."

"Yes, you have a fiancé now. How is everything going with you and Joe?"

"Everything is going great Doctor. He is wonderful and he is everything that I could ever want in a man. He makes me feel loved every day and I can't wait to marry him."

"So you believe that he is the man for you?"

"Yes I do believe that Doctor, but more than anything I believe in who I am now. The person that I have become is nothing like who I used to be. I now know that I deserve to be loved. I never looked at myself the way I do now. I never thought I could love myself or that I even deserved to be loved. Nobody told me I was valuable, nobody told me I was worthy, no man before now had ever shown me love, not even my own father. But most importantly, Nobody Told Me I Was A Queen. This much I know now."

ACKNOWLEDGEMENTS

First of all, I give honor to God who without Him this book would not be possible.

To my husband Roy, thank you for your support and understanding.

To my son Gary, I will always say the same thing to you over and over again. I love you and I am so very proud of you. You got a lot of knowledge for a young dude!

To my youngest son RJ, I am proud to see that you are turning into such a wonderful young man right before our eyes.

To my beautiful girls, you are Queens!

To my grandchildren, may God continue to bless you and always keep you safe.

To my sisters and brothers, I love you and miss you guys.

To my Godmother Barbara, thanks for ALWAYS being there for me.

To my nieces and nephews, I love you all.

To Ebby, I am so proud of you. You are a Queen and don't you ever accept anything less. How was that?

To Dayna, thanks for always being the same person. I can always count on you to never take my side. (Smile) I love you!

To LayNissha, you are more like a daughter to me than anything. I love you and I will always be your *"fairy god mother"*

To Edward Mills, thank you for understanding exactly what I wanted in this book design. I believe people are placed in your life for a reason.

To my dear friend Shannon Myles, you are my little sister and a good friend. I love you and I am glad that you are in my life.

To Dr. Beverly Davis, you are a wonderful woman and I am so happy that I got to know you. You will always be a woman who I look up to and admire.

To all of the young women who attend or have attended ***The Queen's Project***, never forget who you are.

To the great writers who inspire me on a daily basis, Kimberla Lawson Roby, Toni Morrison, Terri McMillan, Maya Angelou and the uplifting writings of Susan Taylor.

To all of the staff at Nellie Stone Johnson Community School in Minneapolis, you guys are a wonderful staff and you do great work. The students are very blessed to have such caring adults watching over them and their education.

And last but not least, to everyone who believed in me and supported my dreams.

Thank you!

PJ Richardson

ABOUT THE AUTHOR

PJ Richardson is a Life Coach and the founder and facilitator of "The Queen's Project". She is a motivational speaker who works to inspire and build self esteem in women of all ages. She is the author of Red Flags and currently working on her third novel. She lives in Brooklyn Park, Minnesota with her husband and business partner. Emails can be sent to: aaqueensproject@yahoo.com